# “Mamie left her h

That was not the subjec
Not with John-Parker.

“Miss Chavez?” The tall, fancy cowboy stood in the center of the room, circling that hat over and over again between his hands, pensive.

She’d give a dollar to know what he was thinking.

“What?” The word was too sharp, and she’d give herself away if she wasn’t careful. No use raising his suspicions.

“Were you and Mamie close?” He seemed to be trying to fit her into his paradigm of Mamie and her foster kids.

He should give up. She didn’t fit. But she didn’t want him to know that.

Zoey stepped away from the staircase.

“In the last year of her life, we became very close. I moved in with her.” She waved one hand. “Long story.”

A story she didn’t want to share with John-Parker Wisdom. She wanted him to get back in his big, fancy pickup, drive back to where he’d been for the last fifteen years and stay there forever.

**Linda Goodnight**, a *New York Times* bestselling author and winner of a RITA® Award in Inspirational Fiction, has appeared on the Christian bestseller list. Her novels have been translated into more than a dozen languages. Active in orphan ministry, Linda enjoys writing fiction that carries a message of hope in a sometimes-dark world. She and her husband live in Oklahoma. Visit her website, lindagoodnight.com, for more information.

**Books by Linda Goodnight**

**Love Inspired**

***House of Hope***

*Redeeming the Past*

***Sundown Valley***

*To Protect His Children*
*Keeping Them Safe*
*The Cowboy's Journey Home*
*Her Secret Son*
*To Protect His Brother's Baby*

***The Buchanons***

*Cowboy Under the Mistletoe*
*The Christmas Family*
*Lone Star Dad*
*Lone Star Bachelor*

**Love Inspired Trade**

*Claiming Her Legacy*

Visit the Author Profile page at LoveInspired.com for more titles.

# REDEEMING THE PAST

## LINDA GOODNIGHT

Recycling programs for this product may not exist in your area.

ISBN-13: 978-1-335-93697-4

Redeeming the Past



For questions and comments about the quality of this book, please contact us at CustomerService@Harlequin.com.



Love Inspired
22 Adelaide St. West, 41st Floor
Toronto, Ontario M5H 4E3, Canada
www.LoveInspired.com

**Printed in Lithuania**

A father of the fatherless, and a
judge of the widows, is God in his holy habitation.
—*Psalms* 68:5

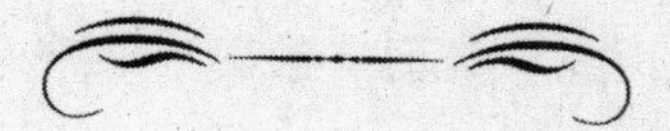

This book is dedicated in memory of super reader,
avid author supporter and all-around
wonderful Christian lady Susan Snodgrass.
We miss you, Susie.

# *Chapter One*

They say you can't go home again.

But could a man go home for the very first time?

John-Parker Wisdom was about to find out.

The rambling, two-story house on a sunshiny lot on Wedgewood Lane looked the same. Mostly. John-Parker spotted a sag here, paint chips there, but the house was still standing.

He'd thought of this place every day since he was an ornery, wayward eighteen-year-old eager to take on the world by himself. Independence day, he'd thought back then.

Now he knew better.

Miss Mamie's house. The house that had built him.

The closest thing to a home he'd known since he was eleven years old, a time so faded in memory, he couldn't conjure his parents' faces. They were an ache, somewhere deep in his soul, that he rarely visited.

Truth was, he didn't often visit any of his past. It hurt too much.

But that was about to change.

He pulled his gleaming blue Dodge Ram to the curb adjacent to the house and killed the engine. His eyes trained on the old structure, his mind tumbled back in time to the first day he'd come here.

Scared, mad, heartsick, and ready to run away.

He shook his head, amused and amazed at how far he'd come. How disciplined he was now, considering how wild he'd been back then. He'd been wilder than the dark tangle of shrubs and woods bordering the creek behind Mamie Bezek's house.

Would Miss Mamie be surprised to see him on her doorstep? Would she even recognize him after fifteen years? From a boy to a man, he'd changed plenty.

He'd planned this day in his head a hundred times. The day when John-Parker Wisdom had made something of himself and returned to make amends.

His gaze roamed the yard. John-Parker frowned, puzzled.

The lawn was empty. A little overgrown. There was no football some boy had forgotten to bring inside. No ancient pickup truck that one of Mamie's street rats was trying to make drivable.

*Street rats*. That's what the small Oklahoma town had called them. Mamie's street rats.

He supposed they had been. But in true rebel fashion, the ornery lot of them had grabbed onto the moniker to wear like a badge of pride. A protective mechanism, he knew now.

The derision had hurt, burrowing deep into each of them until they'd believed the worst of themselves like everyone else. Except for Mamie.

At nearly thirty-four, the moniker still stung John-Parker a little. Not much, but some. The lingering scent of some taints never quite went away.

He squinted around the sparse neighborhood, growing uneasy for reasons he couldn't pinpoint.

Where *were* the kids? The next generation of rowdy boys with trouble in their souls and on their minds. The kids Mamie saved from themselves?

School maybe? Miss Mamie was a stickler for education.

That must be it. School.

John-Parker took his summer Stetson from the passenger seat and clapped it on his head.

Might as well knock on the door and find out.

Hope and a thrill of excitement shimmied through him. Miss Mamie would be over the moon to see him. He was sure of it.

She'd forgive him. He knew she would. All he had to do was ask. She'd wrap her fleshy arms around him and, smelling of talcum powder, she'd welcome him home. Forgiven and loved.

Miss Mamie with her messy mouse-colored bun and twinkling black eyes lived and breathed her faith.

Hopping out of the truck, he did a quick boot check. Shiny brown Ariats. Clean as a whistle.

Miss Mamie said you could tell a lot about a person by their footwear.

Smiling at the memory, he stepped up on the wooden porch with a hollow thud. The weathered boards needed a coat of paint.

Another memory of long ago flashed through his head. A Saturday afternoon when he and Rio had covered the porch and each other with pale blue paint, a mismatch donation from the local hardware store.

"Rio," he murmured.

Over the years and miles, they'd lost touch, this man he'd once considered an almost-brother. He'd looked for Rio, now a man his age, a few times. Nothing. Not even social media. John-Parker prayed that the pretty-boy delinquent hadn't gotten himself killed or sent to prison. Considering Rio's tendency for misbehavior, a tragic end was a definite possibility.

He wondered if Miss Mamie would know where Rio had ended up.

Raising his knuckles, he tapped. Butterflies swirled in his stomach. He refused to believe he was nervous. Excited, yes. Nervous, never. Lives depended on his steel nerves.

Any moment now, he'd see the woman who'd dedicated her life to boys like him. Any moment now, he could begin to right the wrongs he'd done.

He listened, his ear close to the door. Nothing. No sound. Not even the blast of the old-time Southern gospel radio station Mamie favored.

Wasn't she home?

He rapped again and, after another long, disappointing moment, turned to leave. The old door creaked open behind him.

He pivoted, grinning, eager for this moment he'd dreamed of for fifteen years.

"Miss Mamie…" The words died away. This was *definitely* not Miss Mamie.

The young woman standing in the doorway was five and half feet of brunette beneath a straw sunhat tied with yellow ribbons. Her face was…interesting. Not beautiful, but intriguing. Rounded chin, apple cheeks, warmly tanned skin.

"I'm sorry to keep you waiting," she said in a soft tone that sounded sincere. "I was in the garden."

Mamie's vegetable garden. When money was tight or the house too full of kids, she'd planted more and kept them healthy and fed with canned goods from her garden. He'd helped can a quart or two himself in Mamie's kitchen.

"Does Mamie Bezek still live here? Is she home?"

The woman's eyes widened. Her mouth opened, closed, opened again. "No. She's—not here anymore."

The woman untied the ribbons and slid the floppy straw from her head, lowering it to her side. The ribbons trailed against the threshold, sunshine yellow on dark damaged wood. Brown wisps of hair caught the light behind her and danced with static.

"Not here? Did she retire?" That made no sense. This was Mamie's home. If she retired, she'd still be here on Wedgewood Lane. "Can you tell me where to find her?"

The woman's bow lips flat-lined. Two tidy brown eyebrows pulled together in a frown.

"Were you one of her boys?" A pair of onyx eyes pinned to his face.

"Yes, ma'am. I was. I'm John-Parker Wisdom."

The interesting woman turned her head to one side, licked full lips, avoided his gaze.

"John-Parker Wisdom," she repeated softly as if she knew the name. Turning back, barely meeting his eyes, she added, "I'm Zoey Chavez, Mamie's niece."

She didn't invite him in. Rather, she stood there, blocking the doorway with her slender frame, as if he wasn't welcome.

"I didn't know Mamie had a niece." Why hadn't he known that?

"She didn't until..." Zoey Chavez waved one hand.

Until what?

He was starting to have that spider-crawling-up-his-back feeling. The one he got when a security gig was about to turn sour.

Where was Mamie?

John-Parker cleared his throat. "Forgive the intrusion, but I grew up in this house, and I've waited a long time to see Mamie again. Do you mind if come inside for a few minutes? Maybe have a look around the old place for memories' sake while you find her address for me?"

"I don't know you."

"But you recognized my name. Mamie spoke of me, didn't she?"

"Yes, but—"

Had Mamie said something negative about him?

A stab of betrayal found its mark. Mamie had always believed in him. Hadn't she?

"Did Mamie tell you what a punk I was? Is that it? I'm not that guy anymore."

"Mr. Wisdom."

"John. John-Parker."

She tilted her head. Thick brown hair flared out to one side, revealing large, gold, earring hoops. "We'll both be happier in the long run if you go back to wherever you've lived since you left Rosemary Ridge. Waxing nostalgic is a waste of time."

They'd *both* be happier? What did she mean by that?

Something was wrong. He knew it as well as he knew what Mamie had done for him all those years ago.

He blocked the first terrible thought that pinged into his head. *Don't go there.*

Mamie was fine. She'd moved away. Nothing to get twisted about.

In his business, he'd learned persistence. He wasn't leaving without that address.

"I won't stay long. Only long enough to look around a bit and get Mamie's new address."

Zoey gave a heavy sigh and then stepped back, holding the peeling wooden door open so he could enter.

John-Parker ducked beneath the doorframe, a habit from years of ducking ceiling fans and low doorways. A man six feet two inches didn't always fit.

As he stepped inside the living room, he was swamped with nostalgia. The battered old sectional looked the same, but it couldn't be. Could it? Dirty white stuffing spilled from the arms and cushions.

A tired bouquet of fake flowers languished in the center of a scarred wooden coffee table.

John-Parker had played a thousand games at that table. Mostly chess. Mamie had taught all her boys to play, insisting chess was good for the brain.

One time, a new kid had kicked the table and scattered the pieces. Rio had pounded the punk until Mamie had flown into the room to break them apart.

Mamie's things were here. This house still echoed her presence.

But where was Miss Mamie?

"I only have a minute," the niece said. "So, if you want to look around real quick…"

Right. Look around. Then go away.

He got the message.

She glanced toward the stairway. "I need to run upstairs."

"To call the police and ask if I'm a criminal?"

She blinked. Her mouth opened in a silent shock. "Are you?"

"No." Not now anyway. "I'm a security specialist."

He withdrew a business card from his shirt pocket and offered it to her.

She took the elegantly engraved card with her thumb and index finger as if his hands were dirty, read it, and slid it into the side pocket of her long floral skirt. Unimpressed. Okay. Fine. He wasn't all that impressed with her either. She obviously considered him a street rat.

"I'll be right back," she said.

"You'll get that address for me." He didn't ask, another psychological trick he'd learned in business. Don't ask. Tell nicely. Lay out the expectation and leave it hanging in the air. Most people avoid confrontation.

Without replying, Zoey Chavez started up the stairs.

He called after her, mostly to get a reaction. "I promise not to steal anything while you're gone."

When she whirled her head to glare at him over one shoulder, John-Parker smirked.

She didn't trust him. He got that. She didn't know him and she was right not to trust a strange man standing on the stoop. But why toss out power vibes of instant dislike?

During her absence, John-Parker strolled through the house. The eat-in kitchen that had once seemed enormous and fancy to him as a kid now appeared small and outdated. Way outdated.

Worn, faded brown Formica counters. Green-and-white-linoleum floors that had long since given up their pattern. But the solid oak in the cabinets, even though old-fashioned, remained in good repair.

He slid his hand across the long, heavy wooden table where he and at least five other boys had stuffed their faces and fought over the last piece of chicken.

He really wanted to walk around the upstairs sleeping quarters but, considering Mamie's niece was up there and he might frighten her, he decided to remember the rooms as they'd been. Wood floors. Double bunk beds in each bedroom. Two dressers. Not room for much else, but all the items growing boys had needed.

Miss Mamie's room was downstairs, toward the back of the house, so he strolled that way, letting memory take him through the laundry room, the den and to her bedroom.

He paused in the doorway, suddenly feeling awkward about invading Mamie's space.

If Mamie had moved away from here, she'd done so recently. Too much was the same.

His mind rolled through the possibilities.

Was Mamie in a nursing home? Was that it?

But why hadn't the niece simply said so?

A ragged old Bible lay on the nightstand. A Bible that Mamie had read to them each night. No matter how the boys had rolled their eyes and groused, she'd insisted they sit and listen.

The pictures on the wall were the same, too.

The stairs overhead creaked. John-Parker glanced up. The niece was coming down again.

Eager for the address, his long strides took him quickly back to the living room.

As Zoey came into sight, he crossed the room and took a seat on the sectional. The worn springs gave beneath his weight. His backside wasn't more than two inches off the hardwood floor.

He felt a little foolish with his knees in the air and his hat in his hand.

The woman pressed a hand to her lips, needing to laugh but refusing to give in. He wondered why she was afraid to laugh.

"Did you get your fill of nostalgia?" she asked, one hand absently smoothing the side of her skirt.

"Yes, and thank you." He would have casually crossed an ankle over his knee but, from this position, he couldn't. "Didn't steal the good silver either."

She gave him a sharp look. "There is silver, you know. The good stuff."

He knew. Oh, did he ever know.

"Look, Miss Chavez, I've driven a thousand miles to see Mamie. At the risk of being rude—" something he was good at him when necessary, although he preferred diplomacy "—I'm here to see Mamie. If you have her address, I'll take it and get out of your way."

Zoey bounced a fist against her mouth. Once. Twice. Finally, she smacked her lips and huffed a sigh. "I don't know how to tell you this. There's no easy way."

A knowing dread rose, dark as circling black buzzards and more terrible than the first day he'd seen this house. The buzzards that had been circling since the moment she'd told him Mamie no longer lived here.

"Is she sick?" *Please, God, let her only be sick.*

"Not anymore. Aunt Mamie passed away in February."

Zoey watched the change come over John-Parker Wisdom. Disbelief. Grief. Anger.

"She can't be." He jerked up from his near-comical position on a couch that needed to be in the dumpster. She'd see it gone soon. Him, too.

"I'm sorry to be the bearer of such news." Very sorry. The last thing she'd needed was for John-Parker Wisdom to show up now.

What were the odds?

Mamie had waited years for this man to come back. So why now? Now that it was too late for him to do anything but cause trouble.

"What happened?" His expression was stricken, his gray eyes haunted. "She was always so vital."

Zoey battled against feeling sorry for him.

"How long since you've seen her, John-Parker?"

"Fifteen years."

"When was the last time the two of you spoke?"

He sighed. Pinched his bottom lip. "Fifteen years ago."

Exactly the reason he should turn his big truck around and head out of Rosemary Ridge. Though not the only one.

"You haven't spoken to her or kept in touch since you left here fifteen years ago."

Her derisive words weren't a question. They were an accusation.

Some of Aunt Mamie's "kids" sent cards or emails. Some had even returned for a visit. But John-Parker Wisdom hadn't been one of them. Zoey knew because, in her final year, Mamie had worried about him the most.

"I should have, but I needed to..." He shook his head, leaving the thought to dangle in the tense air separating them.

Needed to what?

He gazed up at the high dingy ceiling, his handsome face tragic.

Even though Zoey didn't want to notice, the man *was* good-looking.

He was dressed well in upscale Western style, more like a Dallas businessman than an actual cowboy. He held a white Stetson in one hand. Not a bedraggled work hat, but a pristine Stetson a Western man would wear for dress-up. His brown hair was neatly cut and groomed. A shadow of dark scruff outlined his lower face.

Except for the wide scar running across his thick left eyebrow like a two-lane highway, his sculpted face was near perfection.

*Pretty is as pretty does.*

Zoey practically heard Aunt Mamie speaking in her ear. And her aunt was exactly right.

John-Parker Wisdom might look good on the outside, but his actions had left him woefully lacking.

Where had he been all this time?

And what right did he have to show up now?

Boys like him had taken everything Aunt Mamie had had to give, stolen her adult years, her money, her chances at marriage and a family of her own. They were selfish street rats Mamie had prayed for and grieved.

This one in particular.

*Why, Aunt Mamie? Why him?*

"Was she sick?" His glazed eyes, the color of a cloudy morning, stared unseeing at the squeaky ceiling fan. Five blades emitted a rhythmic squeak as they rotated a lazy breezeless circle. "I don't remember her ever being sick."

Zoey wanted to say her aunt had died of a broken heart, but instead she named the diagnosis. "Cancer."

His teeth bared in a hiss. "I hate cancer."

She scoffed. "Welcome to the universe."

Her sharp tone brought his gaze back to her.

"How long was she sick?" he asked as if the thought of Mamie suffering brought him pain. She could credit him for the compassion if little else.

"Over three years, but she didn't tell anyone until the last year when she was too weak to foster her boys any longer."

His eyes slammed shut. Pain wracked his face. "She went right on fostering teenage throwaways even after she got sick. Yeah. I can see her doing that. As long as she could."

"She shouldn't have. The stress, the financial strain—" Zoey clamped her lips shut.

Blaming John-Parker wouldn't bring Mamie back.

Neither would resentment. But Zoey felt the gnawing fury in every fiber of her being.

The man's eyes settled on her. "Mamie left her house to you?"

That was not the subject Zoey wanted to discuss. Not with him.

She went to the staircase, listening. No sound. They still slept.

"Miss Chavez. Zoey?" The tall, fancy cowboy stood in the center of the room, circling that hat over and over again between his hands, pensive.

She'd give a dollar to know what he was thinking.

"What?" The word was too sharp and she'd give herself away if she wasn't careful. No use raising his suspicions.

"Were you and Mamie close?" He seemed to be trying to fit her into his paradigm of Mamie and her foster kids.

He should give up. She didn't fit. But she didn't want him to know that.

Zoey stepped away from the staircase.

"In the last year of her life, we became very close. I moved in with her." She waved one hand. "Long story."

A story she didn't want to share with John-Parker Wisdom. She wanted him to get back in his big fancy pickup, drive to wherever he'd been for the last fifteen years, and stay there.

Silence dangled between them, a venomous snake.

He shifted on the shiniest brown boots she'd ever seen. Awkward. Unsure. Adjectives she wouldn't have ascribed to the confident man in front of her.

"Well—" When she didn't pick up the conversation, he dipped his chin and moved toward the door. Very astute of him.

"The town has probably changed a lot. Can you recommend a hotel or bed-and-breakfast?"

"You're staying in Rosemary Ridge?" Horror prickled the hairs on her arms.

*No. No. He had to leave!*

The cowboy offered her a look, the kind that said she was a few croutons short of a chef's salad.

"Lady, I'm not driving another thirteen hundred miles without some sleep."

"Oh." She gnawed the inside of her lip.

His eyebrows rose. "Don't look so sad." She clearly didn't. "You don't have to see me again."

"It's not that."

"Yes, it is. Having one of Mamie's street rats show up on your doorstep isn't your idea of a pleasant afternoon of tea and crumpets with friends. My presence might turn the neighbors against you."

He was bitter. But why should she care?

Her conscience twanged, a tuning fork in her ear.

She did care, which could become a serious problem in this situation.

Zoey didn't judge people by their childhoods. She'd be a fool to do that, considering her own destructive upbringing. She judged them by how they behaved as adults.

In her estimation, John-Parker Wisdom had been found guilty and condemned.

Tuning fork or not.

A cry broke from upstairs.

John-Parker Wisdom's head whipped upward so fast, she thought he might suffer whiplash.

"A baby's crying." He spun his head toward her. "You have a baby?"

Another cry joined the first one.

"Yes. Two of them." She ushered him to the door, thankful for her crying children. An excuse to get rid of John-Parker Wisdom. "Wildwood Bed-and-Breakfast on Walker and Seventh. Walker is on a side road off Main—"

"I know where Walker is."

Of course, he did. He'd lived in Rosemary Ridge. Small towns weren't in the habit of changing street names. "Fine. Nice meeting you. Have a safe trip home."

She gave him a not-too-gentle shove out the door and slammed it behind him.

Turning the lock, Zoey rested all of four seconds against the door before racing up the stairs.

John-Parker Wisdom's absence from this house, this town, was the only solution to what had suddenly become a monumental problem.

# *Chapter Two*

John-Parker missed the turn on to Walker Street.

The town had grown and changed, but the differences weren't the problem. His head was.

If he'd returned a few months ago, Mamie would still have been alive. Or if he'd made a phone call or sent a message.

But he hadn't. He'd expected the small town and the life he'd left behind to freeze in place until he was ready to play the big-shot.

He'd wanted to glide into town in his new pickup, flush with money and a successful business, and make her proud. At last. He'd wanted to prove to her and the world that what she'd done for him and the other boys changed lives.

"The best laid plans," he murmured.

Why hadn't he considered the possibility?

Why hadn't he known she had a niece? A niece who, unlike her aunt, had taken one glance at John-Parker and relegated him to the dumpster where rats belong.

He hadn't felt that kind of rejection in a long time. Hadn't realized how much that attitude from people still bothered him. He'd thought it buried and gone. But there it was, too easily resurrected, sharp and gouging into him.

Suddenly, up ahead, a red light flashed. John-Parker recognized the traffic signal and slammed on his brakes in time to stop.

When had Rosemary Ridge put up traffic lights?

He blew out a long breath, relieved not to have been T-boned by the semi roaring through the intersection.

He shouldn't be driving. He wasn't focused. A heavy fog covered his brain, his eyes, his heart.

Flipping on his blinker, he pulled into a parking spot

against the curb. In front of him was a row of businesses. A boutique, a coffee shop, a newspaper office.

Only the newspaper office was the same. The boutique and coffee shop were new. To him, at least.

He squinted down the street. Was that a café on the corner where the drugstore had been?

He could grab some coffee, a bite to eat, maybe a local paper to see if he recognized anyone or anything. Something to occupy his mind other than his utter complete failure. A failure he couldn't rectify. Ever.

His cell phone rang and he pulled it from his pocket to answer.

His business partner, Brandt James.

"Hey." He sighed into the speaker.

"You don't sound too chipper. Did you make it to Miss Mamie's place yet?"

"Yeah."

"And? Was she thrilled to see your ugly mug?"

"She's dead."

The shocked silence on the end hummed in John-Parker's ear.

"No way," Brandt finally whispered. "Not Miss Mamie."

"My thoughts exactly. She got cancer a couple of years ago. Died last February." His throat thickened with the emotion he didn't want to feel. "I missed seeing her by three months."

He should have returned to Rosemary Ridge at Christmas. He'd planned to. But then business had called him to Buenos Aires to protect an American senator and he'd spent Christ's birthday sweating like a pig and praying the fireworks weren't a cover for gunfire.

If only he'd sent one of the other security specialists.

Silence stretched again. There were no words. Brandt knew how important today's trip had become to him.

A chance at absolution, at redemption by the one person he wanted it from.

"What are you going to do now?" Brandt's voice was low and gentle. "Head back to Phoenix?"

John-Parker didn't like needing that gentleness. "Don't know yet. My mind is still reeling."

He'd throw himself into work, probably. That's what he always did.

"Yeah. Mine, too. I'd offer to come down there, but—"

"I know." Brandt would rather walk on burning glass than set foot in Rosemary Ridge again. Some hurts burrow so deep that a man runs instead of facing them. Not that he'd ever say that to Brandt. His friend had the courage of ten men, except when it came to Rosemary Ridge.

They were both emotion avoiders in their own way. Their cool-under-pressure façades worked well in the bodyguard business.

"Maybe I'll stick around a day or two. Rest up, find out where she's buried and take her some flowers."

"Wild ones were her favorites." Brandt's words ached with the memory.

"Fitting, don't you think? Wild boys. Wildflowers. Remember how she loved dandelions and wanted them to cover the lawn? 'Spots of sunshine,' she called them." He allowed a soft nostalgic smile. "She found a way to see the best in the things other people considered useless."

Like him and Brandt and dozens of others.

"Good woman. Not many of those left."

John-Parker rubbed fatigue from the back of his neck. He couldn't name even one woman Brandt trusted, except for Miss Mamie. He worked with them, protected them in his job, but held them all at arm's length.

Lots of baggage in Brandt James's closet.

John-Parker wasn't a man given to tears but, at times like these, he wished he was. Crying might relieve the pressure in his chest, the wound that seemed to fester by the minute.

He was too late. Mamie was dead. God may have forgiven him, but Mamie never would.

"How's work?" he asked, eager for the distraction of business. "Any problems?"

"None so far."

"Steve back from Guatemala yet?"

"Yesterday. He's taking a few days off."

As specialists providing protection to executives, politicians and other bigwigs, their company, Silent Security, worked all over the world. He and Brandt owned the firm but hired hand-picked, military-trained bodyguards and computer security operatives, adding more as the business expanded. Though their home base was Phoenix, they could work from anywhere. And often did.

Since leaving Mamie's house to join the military, he and Brandt had logged a lot of miles and built a strong reputation as some of the best in the personal security business.

Somehow through the mess of their childhoods, they'd become brothers, though they didn't share a drop of DNA.

Brandt was the only family John-Parker had. He'd once have included Rio in that family. Guess Rio didn't feel the same. Neither John-Parker nor Brandt had heard from him since they'd left the military.

A fire truck wailed past, blowing a fog horn as it blasted through the traffic light and waking John-Parker from his thoughts.

"I'm going to grab some breakfast. Call me if anything comes up."

"Don't worry. I'll hold the fort."

John-Parker knew that. He'd trust Brandt with his life. In fact, he had more than once.

He pressed the red phone icon and ended the call.

Heart heavy, he exited the truck and stepped up on the sidewalk. Cars passed behind him with a quiet swish of tires on pavement. Another approached from the south, muffler too loud.

Two elderly men, one taller than John-Parker and the other

short and wiry, exited the newspaper office, arguing over something.

John-Parker logged all the activity, every person who came and went on the street, the three slamming car doors, the voices: two women and a man, a burst of laughter.

Awareness of absolutely everything was his business. Missing the slightest thing could get a client—and him—killed.

He'd missed something at Mamie's house. He was sure of it because of the niggle at the back of his neck, the slight tingle that said all was not as it should be.

Or was that only the grief creeping in on panther paws, ready to rip his heart out?

"Howdy there, son, you looking for something?" The speaker was an angular elderly man in denim overalls, with a hawk nose and a battered plaid fedora atop thinning gray hair.

The gentleman with him, a wiry cowboy type no taller than a twelve-year-old, put in his two cents' worth. "Reason my brother is poking his long nose in your business is 'cause you look lost. Are you new in town?"

"In a manner of speaking. I lived here a long time ago."

"Ah, well then, welcome back. I'm Wink Myrick and my brother here is Frank." He stuck out a hand.

John-Parker gave the hand a shake. For a little man, Wink's grip was surprisingly strong. "John-Parker Wisdom."

The taller one, Frank, frowned. "Name sounds familiar, but when you get close to eighty years on this planet, you think you probably know everyone in the world but you forgot half of them." He chuckled. "So what can we do for you, John-Parker Wisdom? If you're hunting up old friends, we likely know 'em."

"Yep. We know everybody. You don't get this old in a town this small without knowing every soul. Some of them twice." The cowboy laughed at his own joke.

John-Parker had no intention of airing his past or his heartache over Mamie with anyone, no matter how friendly they were.

"Can you recommend a good place to get a bite to eat?"

The two exchanged glances. "That's what we were arguing about when we seen you drive up. Wink here wants one of them fancy muffins and a cappuccino from that fancy-pants coffee shop." Frank jerked a thumb toward the Daily Grind next door. "A working man like me needs real food like they got down at the Drugstore Café."

Wink huffed. "You ain't worked a full day in six years."

The bigger one, Frank, snorted. "What would you know about work? All you do is ride that old horse and play cowboy."

Wink poked out his chest and rose to a full five feet and two inches, if John-Parker was guessing right. "I don't play cowboy. I *am* a cowboy. Who do you think raises that steak you like to eat?"

While the two brothers bickered, John-Parker held back a grin. One thing about the pair, they took his mind off his troubles.

"Excuse me, fellas. I hate to interrupt, but I think I'll step inside here and grab a newspaper." He dipped his head, politelike. "Good to meet you."

As he reached for the handle on the glass door of the newspaper office, he heard the argument start up again.

"See? Now you done run the poor boy off. What kind of welcome to Rosemary Ridge is that?"

"I didn't run him off. You did with all that blathering about cappuccinos and muffins. Couldn't you tell he's a bacon-and-egg man? Probably likes meatloaf, too."

John-Parker let the grin come.

The inside of the newspaper office smelled like new books and ink. He paused at the long counter, the wood scarred. Newspapers stacked on one end.

A slim woman with *I Love Lucy* hair piled atop her head rose from a messy paper-laden desk and came to greet him. "May I help you?"

"Just need a newspaper and some information."

She smiled. "Information is my business. And you, sir, look very familiar. Did we, by chance, attend high school together?"

An almost-forgotten name clicked in John-Parker's brain. "Clare Valandingham?"

She'd been the brain in his sophomore English class. The girl who'd written essays and poems and won a trip to Washington, DC, through the local electrical co-op for her essay on renewable energy.

"That's me. And you are— Don't tell me." She tapped a finger against her cheek as she studied his face. "Oh, I hate when I can't remember a name. Your face is so familiar."

"John-Parker Wisdom. I think we had English together." He braced himself for disdain while hoping for something better, praying she didn't remember the times he'd mocked her poetry or hassled the teacher over assignments he hadn't done.

"That's right. We did! Mrs. Haney's sophomore English."

He released a pent-up breath. Clare, with the two pencils and one pen stuck in various places through her curly red hair, gave no sign that he'd done anything back then to earn her derision. "One and the same."

"So, tell me, John-Parker Wisdom, what are you doing back in Rosemary Ridge?" She smiled again. Friendly, nosy maybe, but not flirty. She was a journalist, so, of course, she was curious.

"I came to see an old friend only to learn that she's passed away. Maybe you have her obituary in your archives? I'd like a copy."

"If you know the date and name, I can find her for you."

He gave her the information and, after slanting him a quiet, knowing look, she whipped around, stick-thin in straight dress slacks and a fitted suit jacket, to a laptop computer opened on her messy desk.

If she remembered he was one of Mamie's street rats, she was polite enough not to mention that fact.

While he waited, John-Parker let his eyes roam the space.

A man typed away at a laptop in one corner of the room. Through a glass divider, he spotted a gangly youth with an orange mohawk, maybe sixteen, and a middle-aged woman with heavy black glasses.

The place was so similar to the way it had been years ago, he almost expected to see Buster Tripp stumble from the back with ink on his nose and fingers, blinking like a gopher on Groundhog Day.

Instead, the red-haired Clare scribbled something on a notepad and carried it toward the glass divider. "Herbie, will you look up this paper, please?"

The mohawk-wearing teen took the note and disappeared around a wall.

"I'll take today's paper, too," John-Parker said, drawing his wallet from his back pants' pocket.

Clare took his money. "Mamie Bezek was a lovely person. We were all sad to learn of her death."

"Yeah." He didn't know what else to say. If he started talking about Mamie now, he might fold. And he wasn't a man who folded.

Herbie returned with a paper in hand.

Without looking through the pages for the obituary, something he wanted to do in private, John-Parker folded the two newspapers under one arm.

"Does the Drugstore Café make a decent breakfast?" he asked.

"An excellent breakfast." Clare glanced at her watch—a fitness tracker, as if she needed to lose a few pounds. "Closer to lunch now, but they serve breakfast all day, if that's what you want. The cook is a trained chef. Used to cook for a major hotel in New Orleans. He's very good."

John-Parker wasn't looking for fancy, just tasty, but he thanked the informative newspaperwoman and headed out the door.

So far, so good. The people he'd encountered hadn't run screaming the moment they'd heard his name.

Maybe time did heal old wounds or, at least, fade memories. Theirs anyway.

Whatever. He could relax a little and stop waiting for someone to recognize his name and call the cops or scream in his face about what a worthless street rat he was.

With the May sun warm and pleasant, he walked the half block to the corner café. The scent of bacon greeted him before he opened the door and stepped inside.

Voices rose around him, the chatter of friends catching up on a Tuesday morning. Dishes clattered, chairs scraped as John-Parker cased the room. Most of the tables and booths were full. A long counter that he remembered as a soda fountain ran the length of one side. Half the stools were empty.

He started in that direction when a voice called his name. He followed the sound to one of the old men he'd met earlier—Wink, the short cowboy—waving at him. "We've got room at our table."

*Why not?* John-Parker thought, and wove his way through the sea of diners to join the Myrick brothers.

A waitress brought water and a menu, and he ordered the lunch special, mostly to get a reaction from the Myrick brothers. Clare was right. It would soon be noon, close enough to have the meatloaf and mashed potatoes.

"See there, Wink, I told you he was a meatloaf man, and Catfish makes the best you ever ate." The latter he aimed at John-Parker.

"You eat here often?" John-Parker asked to make conversation.

"Too often," Wink grumbled. "Frank here thinks we have to patronize the place because our brother is the cook. I don't get why we need to pay Catfish to cook for us when he does it for free at home."

"The boy has to make a living," Frank said as he stirred three packets of Splenda into his coffee.

"So your brother is the fancy chef from New Orleans?" John-Parker asked, amused by the bickering brothers.

"One and the same. He's retired now."

While John-Parker pondered this bit of oxymoron, a burly server returned to top off coffee mugs and refill iced-tea glasses—a pitcher in one hand and a carafe in the other.

"Catfish says he'll be out in a minute with Wink's muffins."

The waiter had no more than said the words before a man who clearly loved his own cooking exited through the swinging double doors and barreled toward them, strings of his white apron flapping behind him.

He slid a plate full of richly scented blueberry muffins onto the table. Topped with some sort of crunchy-looking crumbs, delicate stripes of icing fancied them up.

"Help yourself, boys." The cook's gaze, as black and small as raisins in a fluffy loaf of white bread, landed on John-Parker. "Who's this?"

"Catfish Myrick, meet John-Parker Wisdom. He used to live here and he's back to visit."

The chef's hefty brow folded accordion-style. "John-Parker Wisdom. You must be here about the inheritance."

John-Parker blinked once. Twice. "The inheritance?"

Frank snapped his fingers. "That's it. I knew I'd heard your name recently. Mamie Bezek's will. The lawyer's been looking for you."

John-Parker tried to keep his expression bland but his insides were going crazy. He had no idea what the men were talking about. No one, not one person, had contacted him about a will.

Miss Mamie had left a will that mentioned him?

Zoey Chavez must have known.

But she hadn't said a word.

"Mr. Wisdom." Zoey kept her tone as cool as the cucumbers she'd planted this morning in the backyard garden, but her first instinct was to slam the door in his face.

"John-Parker." The man ground out the words between his teeth. "We need to talk."

Dread, worry, fear knotted up in her gut. Apparently, he'd learned something. He certainly hadn't gone away, like she'd hoped.

He didn't wait for her to invite him in. He pushed the door open with one very strong hand and stormed past her. He was hatless this time, as if in too big of a hurry to bother with the Stetson.

If he didn't radiate hot waves of anger, she'd have enjoyed looking at him. Foolish female that she was. A good-looking man wasn't necessarily a good one.

Certainly not this man.

She calmly closed the door behind him and put herself between him and the two little ones playing with stacking toys on a quilt beside the couch. Her pulse was in overdrive.

He stacked a hand on each hip, his sleek gray suit jacket flared out at the sides.

Zoey braced herself, ready to fight, though the tall, muscular man outweighed her by plenty and was twice her bulk. She couldn't run, not with her children in the room.

She glanced around for a weapon, landing on the sad vase of flowers on the coffee table. The glass jar wasn't much, but any weapon was better than nothing.

"What do you want?" she asked, annoyed that her voice trembled.

John-Parker's gaze flashed to the little ones. Owen raised his three-year-old head and stared with dark brown eyes at the newcomer. "Hi. I'm Owen."

Zoey's heart squeezed. Her boy loved people.

Some of the fury seeped out of John-Parker. "Hi, Owen. What's your sister's name?"

"Livia. She's a baby."

Olivia, too small to feel the tension, went right on stacking colorful rings.

The cowboy's fury tempered. Not fully, but a little.

"Cute kids."

"Thank you." Now, please leave.

Returning his attention to her, John-Parker took a deep breath, let it out, relaxing those broad shoulders.

"All right, look." He stretched out both hands, palms down. "I heard something in town I need to ask you about."

Maybe he wasn't a monster. Maybe they could carry on a decent conversation without violence.

Not that she trusted any man not to hit first and talk later.

She moved closer to the vase just in case.

"What did you hear?" She hoped with everything in her that there was another explanation for him coming back to Mamie's house.

"Did you know about Mamie's will?"

Her heart tumbled to the hardwood floor and lay there, floundering like a banked perch.

He knew.

# *Chapter Three*

As far as John-Parker knew, Buckner and Buckner had provided law services for Rosemary Ridge since statehood. And the interior of their offices looked as if they hadn't changed much since that momentous shift from Indian Territory to Oklahoma in 1907.

A secretary, whose desk nameplate read Joan, greeted him in the entry and ushered him through a doorway into a typical office loaded with plenty of dark wood. Book-lined shelves along the back wall, an executive desk in the center lit by a large window on the left, and a scattering of padded office chairs. An American flag stood proudly in one corner next to an Oklahoma Sooner football banner.

He settled in one of the maroon chairs. Zoey had not yet arrived, which was good. Her tardiness gave him a minute to collect his thoughts.

Not that he'd thought of much else since learning two days ago about some kind of inheritance. Though he'd blown into Buckner's office after demanding the truth from Zoey, he'd learned exactly nothing. The lawyer had insisted on waiting until "the appointed time" to reveal the contents of Mamie's will.

The door opened and he knew without looking that Zoey had arrived. The tension in the room shot up like a last-second three-pointer from midcourt.

She chose the chair farthest away from him. He turned to stare at her, still upset that she'd intended to let him drive away from Rosemary Ridge without so much as telling him of Mamie's will.

To his knowledge, all Mamie owned was the house and the lots around it. Granted, those would bring a nice amount in today's booming market, but money wasn't an issue for him. Besides, he figured Mamie had left the house to Zoey, though the sneaky woman with the doe eyes had neither confirmed nor denied the fact.

He didn't want Mamie's house. He didn't want anything material from her. He only wanted forgiveness, redemption. Surely, if she had mentioned him in the will, she'd left some final parting words. Something to assuage his aching conscience.

That's why he'd stuck around, why he hadn't simply driven away and left behind the annoying, if intriguing, Miss Zoey Chavez and her secrets.

The attorney aimed a smile at John-Parker. "You, sir, are a difficult man to track down."

"I shouldn't be. My business is public." He shifted in the chair, gripping the arms. "That's what I don't understand. It seems someone may not have wanted me to know about this will." He turned an icy glare toward Zoey.

"Then, sir, you should check with whoever answers the phone at your offices. I've left several messages."

John-Parker sat back, shocked at the news. "I travel a lot."

"So I learned." Buckner shifted a folder. "Nonetheless, you're here, as is Miss Chavez, and just in the nick of time."

"The nick of time for what?"

"For this reading. According to Miss Bezek's directives, if you weren't found by the last day of May, Miss Chavez inherited everything."

John Parker turned yet another frigid glare on the woman. She sat with her head down, fingers clutching each other as if they were about to fly off her hands.

The dishonest, underhanded, conniving little sneak. She'd probably hoodwinked a sick and dying Mamie, coerced her by worming her way into Mamie's life and pretending to care. All for a house. If she had, John-Parker Wisdom would fight her to his dying breath.

"I see," he said, though he really didn't. "Are we the only

two people mentioned in the will? Or are there others who weren't found?"

"Besides a few incidentals to a handful of others, which are not your concern, the primary heirs to Mamie Bezek's estate are John-Parker Wisdom and Zoey Alaina Chavez."

Shock ricocheted down his spine. "Why?"

"That's something Miss Bezek preferred to remain private." The attorney tilted his head. "For now."

Meaning what?

"Could we get on with the reading?" Zoey's voice was barely above a whisper. "I need to get back to my children. They're with a friend, but I don't like to impose for too long." She stared straight ahead at the attorney, avoiding John-Parker's glare.

He was aware of her in the most uncomfortable way. She intrigued, even attracted him, but now that he knew of her deception, at least in part, resentment and anger warred like gladiators in his chest.

She must have coerced Mamie, which would explain her inclusion.

But the bigger question remained. Why him?

Mr. Buckner cleared his throat. "Let's begin."

Zoey felt the daggers John-Parker Wisdom shot at her. Every one of them. All the way to her bone marrow.

Sweat gathered on the back of her neck, though cooled air floated down from a ceiling vent.

Mr. Buckner rambled out a number of legalities she didn't fully understand or care about. She was waiting for him to get down to business, though she felt like a vulture for wanting to hear that Mamie had left her the house.

The older woman had treated her like a daughter. Because of her friendship with Zoey's late grandmother, Mamie had taken her in when she'd been a widowed mother, broke, scared and homeless...and pregnant with yet a second child, a child she could not support.

She owed Mamie Bezek her life and that of her children. Mamie was the rescuer, the giver.

Though Zoey had nursed her through the last horrible months of her life, the care she'd given was nothing compared to all that Mamie had done for her. If she had her way, Mamie would still be alive, and Zoey would have taken care of her for another hundred years.

"'To Zoey Alaina Chavez and John-Parker Wisdom, I leave my earthly possessions other than those designated herein, including but not limited to, the house and land at 508 Wedgewood Lane in Rosemary Ridge, Oklahoma, and all its contents, with the following restrictions and stipulations.'"

The lawyer looked up from the will and adjusted his reading glasses. "I'll paraphrase the rest and leave out the legalese. In summary, except for a handful of bequests whose beneficiaries shall remain anonymous for now, Mamie wanted the two of you to inherit the bulk of her estate jointly."

"Jointly? With *him*?" The words burst from Zoey's throat as shockwaves rolled through her. "Jointly with a man who couldn't even be bothered to come to Mamie's funeral? We don't even know each other!"

The attorney lowered a look of mild reproof. "Let me finish. The property and certain other financial considerations are held in joint trust, to be executed by Lonnie Buckner, attorney-at-law, for the period of three months."

"Wait. Whoa. Mamie didn't have any other financial considerations. She spent all her money on fostering." The glance John-Parker shot her would have frozen a forest fire. "And, apparently, on this woman and her two kids."

Anger bubbled to the surface. Zoey didn't bother to fight it. "How dare you accuse me when all you and your kind ever did was take from her?"

A momentary flare of pain flashed across John-Parker's face before his stormy eyes went cold and hard.

She'd hurt him.

Her conscience panged. Even if her words were true, she

was rarely ever that blunt and cruel. But her babies' future was at stake. She'd do anything for them, even put up with *him* for a few months. Yet the question nagged at her. Why would Mamie expect such a thing? Why him?

The dignified attorney held up a palm. "Mr. Wisdom, Miss Chavez, if you'll let me finish, I'll be glad to allow the two of you to vent any and all frustrations and questions."

Embarrassed by her outburst, Zoey settled, her hands white-knuckling the chair arm. She couldn't look at John-Parker Wisdom. "I apologize, Mr. Buckner. I'm terribly confused by all this."

"Hopefully, I can clear things up for you. Both of you must decide together what to do with your joint inheritance. The property cannot be sold or given away for the full three months beginning June first. This time frame gives you plenty of time to calm down, think clearly and make rational decisions. Once the three months expires, during which you are expected to improve upon the aging home with the accompanying funds, you must agree *jointly*—" he emphasized the word as if he suspected neither Zoey nor John-Parker wanted to agree on anything "—on exactly what's to be done with the property."

"All right. Fine." John-Parker gripped the wooden chair arms as he started to rise. "My decision is made and I'm sure Miss Chavez will agree. No need to wait three months." He didn't bother to look at her. "She can have everything."

Zoey's heart jumped. A thrill of hope and joy rushed through every cell in her body. If the fake cowboy forfeited his right to Mamie's property, everything would be hers. She and the babies would be saved.

If she believed in the goodness of God the way Aunt Mamie had, she would have thanked Him.

Her problems were over, courtesy of the most unlikely person. She should probably thank him, but she couldn't quite bring herself to that point.

She couldn't forget how Mamie had longed to see him

again. Why him? Why not the other boys? She'd asked herself that question a thousand times. Had even asked Mamie. And she still didn't know.

But that was not important today.

Just as she was speculating on how perfect life would be when John-Parker Wisdom left town of his own accord and the house on Wedgewood would be hers to fix up and sell, the attorney waved the man back down.

"That's not possible, Mr. Wisdom. The property cannot transfer for the allotted period. Furthermore, both you and Miss Chavez must reside in Rosemary Ridge during those three months."

John-Parker shook his head. He looked frazzled, stunned and sad, but Zoey refused to feel sorry for him.

"Not happening," he said. "I have a business to run and a busy life in Phoenix. I can't stay. Sorry."

*Good. Go away.*

"You might want to rethink your decision, Mr. Wisdom. If either of you forfeits, you both lose everything."

"No!" Zoey leaped from her chair. How had she gone from hope to terror in so short a time? "That's not fair. If he leaves town, my children and I suffer *his* consequences? That's so wrong! Mamie wouldn't do that to us."

"My job is to inform you of Miss Bezek's last wishes. You can always fight this in court, but would you want to do that to a woman who obviously loved you both and must have had a purpose in writing such a will?"

Zoey sat down again, fuming.

"I can't believe Mamie wanted this," she said to the lawyer. "Are you sure you didn't talk her into such a strange idea?"

While the attorney looked appropriately offended as any reputable attorney would, Zoey felt John-Parker shift toward her. She didn't want to look at him, but he seemed to compel her gaze toward him.

His gray eyes were the color of a stormy sky. Right before a tornado. "Are you sure *you* didn't coerce her, Miss Chavez?"

Zoey glared back. "What is that supposed to mean?"

His nostrils flared in distaste. "A sick woman, especially one with Mamie's kind heart, would be sympathetic toward a young mother all alone with two little ones. All it would take was a little pressure, a few carefully placed hints."

Hackles rose on the back of Zoey's neck.

"I never asked Mamie for anything. She was the one who offered." Zoey crossed her arms over her pounding heart, struggling for control. *That man. That man.* He infuriated her with his innuendoes and outright accusations. "I *loved* her and, except for the needs of my children, I wouldn't care about anything other than a few photos and keepsakes."

"Then, Miss Chavez," the attorney said over his readers in a firm tone intending to calm and persuade, "you'll have to trust that Mamie loved you in return and that she knew exactly what she was doing."

Zoey opened her mouth but closed it again. What could she say to refute that? Mamie had been competent and mentally sharp right up until the end. Her aunt had had a reason for making such a will as this.

She wished she knew what that reason was.

A rustle of motion came from her right. Shiny boots rubbed lightly against the carpet.

"I'll have to think and pray about this." John-Parker rose from his chair. "Thank you, Mr. Buckner. I'll be in touch."

"Don't take too long."

"Right. A day or two."

"Understandable." The two men shook hands and, without so much as a parting glance at her, John-Parker walked out of the office.

Zoey glared at the empty spot he'd left, the scent of his aftershave in her nose.

He'd have to *pray* about it? Well, if that wasn't the most hypocritical thing she'd ever heard.

If God cared one whit about any of them, Mamie wouldn't

have suffered. The woman had been as near to perfect as any human being could be.

If God cared, Mamie would still be here alive and well. And John-Parker Wisdom would crawl back under his rock and stay there.

Now, she was stuck with him.

For three miserable months.

*If* he stayed in town.

And if he didn't?

She'd be back on the streets.

Only this time she'd have a baby on each hip and no Mamie to turn to.

# *Chapter Four*

Zoey Chavez's accusations burned inside John-Parker. She'd made him feel small and worthless. Two self-esteem killers he'd fought against all his life.

He'd become a confident businessman, a bodyguard who feared nothing. Then one small gold-digger in a colorful dress had cut him down to size.

Words stung, no matter how many times through his teen years Miss Mamie had reminded him to find his value in Christ, not in someone's hateful words.

He hadn't understood then, had been too rebellious to want anything to do with a wimpy Jesus preaching kindness and love. Which showed how foolish he'd been. There was nothing weak about a man who'd offer himself up as a sacrifice for others.

Even now that he understood what Mamie had meant, Zoey's jab still went deep, to a protected place he covered with a veneer of confidence and success.

Fifteen years, and the vulnerability remained. Though safely hidden from the world, that one insecurity still lurked like a ghoul in the darkness, waiting to get him.

Shaking his troubled head, John-Parker paced the bedroom of his small room rental at the Wildwood Bed and Breakfast. From the east wall where a maple headboard pressed against light gray paint to the sunset painting on the west wall was precisely nine of his size-ten steps.

Details. Precision. He prided himself on both.

"Lord, this is a dilemma I didn't see coming." He, who planned every detail of a security gig right down to cameras in the table centerpieces or the number of seconds required to move a client to safety, had been blindsided.

He went through all the arguments in his head. Reasons he couldn't remain in Rosemary Ridge for more than week much less three full months. Mostly professional reasons, but his security business was everything to him. He had a smattering of friends he saw now and then, a church and an apartment to come back to after an assignment. But other than best buddy Brandt, he had no person particularly close, no woman waiting at the door to greet him with a hug and kiss.

He'd never had that. Why think of it now?

Eventually, his thoughts circled back around to Zoey Chavez and her two little kids.

She was in a bad spot. If he left town, she got nothing. Did he even care? Hadn't he wondered if she'd pressured Miss Mamie into this bizarre inheritance?

But if Mamie had truly intended the woman to have an inheritance, wouldn't his refusal be another black spot on his conscience? Another imbedded claw scraping a hole in his soul that he could never fix?

The unanswered questions didn't sit well in his gut. Wishing for an antacid, he rubbed a hand over his blue dress shirt, felt the flat abs that needed a good workout. *Stay in shape. Stay alert. Stay alive.* Wasn't that what he told his employees?

The business needed him. He'd booked a security detail in Chicago this weekend that would take every skill he possessed to protect the highly controversial, wrath-inducing speaker. That's why he'd assigned himself to the detail.

He couldn't remain in this town for more than a few days, much less three miserable months.

*What about Miss Mamie? Didn't you come here to please her?*

That little voice in his head, the one he attributed to the Lord, because he sure hadn't heard it until he'd accepted Jesus, tapped at him.

"Yes, but she's not here anymore." Admitting that she was gone filled his throat again.

*What of her legacy?*

He pondered the thought for a moment. Mamie's legacy was nothing more than an outdated house in a small town that no one had ever heard of.

But was it? Hadn't she spent her entire adult life trying to make a difference? Wasn't what she'd done more of a legacy than an old house?

He could almost hear her voice in his head telling the oft-repeated tale of the child and the starfish; a reminder that every individual was worth the effort to save.

"Each of us is a starfish, John-Parker," she'd say. "Sometimes we get stranded on the beach, and all we need is one willing person to guide us back to the ocean."

He and his foster brothers had been those stranded starfish and she'd guided them as much as they'd let her.

He wished more than anything that she was here to see the changes in him, all because of her and her devotion to God and people. She'd guided him toward the Lord and he'd finally realized that true freedom and safety lay at Jesus's feet, not in his own might.

"Do the right thing, John-Parker," she'd told him so many times, particularly after he'd butted heads with someone. "Treat people the way Jesus did."

Selfishness had made more sense. Do to others *before* they do to you, not as you'd *want* them to do. He'd wrestled with that command plenty in the years before embracing the faith his foster mother had cherished.

His relationship with God had changed his negative attitude.

Today, he wished it hadn't. He wished he could walk away and not care one bit what happened to Zoey Chavez and her kids.

How many boys had he known, though, who had been dumped, rejected, ignored by the people who were supposed to love them the most?

What if Zoey Chavez was innocent—a woman going through a rough patch who'd honorably cared for a dying woman? What if Mamie had freely intended to leave her niece an inheritance, the exact way she'd done for him?

Him. John-Parker Wisdom, a ragtag street rat. Mamie had no idea that he'd turned his life around. Another grief he'd have to bear forever.

Yet she'd left him an inheritance.

And that begged the question. Why him? How could Mamie have cared about him after the way he'd hurt her? And what did she expect him to do with her gift?

Though her verbal attack had stung worse than a bullet, Zoey was right. He'd done nothing to deserve so much as a mention from Miss Mamie.

He leaned both hands against the sill of a window that looked out on a flower garden—another reminder of his foster mother…and her niece.

The evidence loomed large. Mamie Bezek had loved him unconditionally. No matter his sins, she'd gone on loving him. She must have felt the same about Zoey Chavez.

Collapsing on the brocade armchair next to the window, he squeezed finger and thumb against the bridge of his nose. His eyes burned. A knot of grief thickened his throat.

"Oh, Mamie," he groaned. "Forgive me."

He didn't know how long he sat there, letting grief rake his insides. Aware only on the perimeter of his brain of the quiet hum of the HVAC system and the clean scent of the plug-in air freshener against one wall, he began to pray.

He had no answers of his own. He needed God's wisdom.

When nothing came to him other than the memory of two, small, dark-haired children playing sweetly together on a worn rug, he sighed in defeat, took out his phone and called the lawyer's office.

"Buckner and Buckner Law Offices."

He identified himself. "Can you tell me where Mamie Bezek is buried?"

"I'm sorry, Mr. Wisdom," the receptionist said, "I don't know for certain, but with only one cemetery in the area, her grave shouldn't be hard to find. You might try city hall. They keep the cemetery records."

"Thanks." He hung up, only slightly better off than before. For some reason, he felt compelled to see the place where Mamie rested.

Grabbing his truck keys, he headed downtown, cruising until he spotted Mary's Flowers and Gifts, another shop new to him.

After buying a giant wreath and a bouquet of roses, he drove to the sprawling cemetery east of town.

As he parked and exited the truck to stroll the grounds in search of Mamie's headstone, he recalled the times he'd driven here with her and waited in her silver minivan while she'd strolled around the tombstones, stopping now and then to tuck a flower, add an American flag, straighten a tilted vase.

A labor of love, she'd called her devotion to keeping the graves looking nice.

He'd asked her once if she had family buried there. She'd never given him a solid answer. "We're all the family of God, John-Parker."

His search took a while and by the time he found the headstone, perspiration beaded on his forehead. Late May was a fickle month in Oklahoma. Hot and stormy one day, temperate and glorious the next.

The stone was simple, modest, like the woman buried there. Nothing fancy. A small, ordinary, gray granite. He wondered who'd had it placed. Zoey? The lawyer? Mamie's church?

He wished it had been him. He'd have purchased a giant one in shiny black granite that reached halfway to the sky. A monument to the greatest person he'd ever known.

Propping the wreath against the little stone, he went to his haunches with the roses.

"I'm here, Miss Mamie. Me. John-Parker." The burning

ache started in his chest. "I should have come sooner. I didn't know. I wish I'd known."

Not knowing was a weak excuse and Mamie wouldn't approve. Truth and responsibility, she'd insist, no excuses. As kind as she had been, she'd been tough, too. She'd nail a lie to the wall and smash it with a hammer. A weaker woman could never have handled six to eight ornery teenage boys.

Tracing his fingers over her name, John-Parker read the inscription beneath her birth and death dates.

*Bearing much fruit. John 5:8.*

He'd have to look that one up, but he got the gist. He and all the boys who'd benefited from her compassion had been the fruits of her life.

She'd died not knowing he'd become one of the good apples, no longer rotting on the vine.

He could never make it up to her. The ache dug deeper in his chest, a spreading fire of guilt and regret.

"You were right about Jesus. Best friend I ever had. Brandt concurs." He smiled, knowing how thrilled she would have been. She'd have thrown both hands in the air and shouted hallelujah a couple of times before grabbing them in a bear hug.

"Yeah, both of us scoundrels."

He spent a minute telling her about his life, his business partnership with Brandt, and a few of the many places he'd traveled as a security expert.

"I wanted to make you proud. Now there's nothing I can do."

*Oh, but there is.*

The words were not audible but seemed to come from outside him, on the wind maybe, with the fragrance of evergreens, or in the white cloud puffs against the blue sky.

*Zoey.* The wind seemed to sigh the woman's name.

Imagination? Guilt? Probably, but Mamie must have wanted him back in Rosemary Ridge. She'd wanted him to encounter Zoey Chavez.

Or had she?

The worry about the situation surrounding the will and Zoey's involvement nagged at him.

But as he talked to both Mamie and God, one thing became clear. Mamie had borne good fruit. The house she'd left him, run-down as it was, had borne good fruit. Mamie's rambling old two-story was a house of hope for abandoned boys.

Wouldn't she want that legacy to continue?

Was that what she wanted him to understand from her curious bequests?

The more he thought about it, the more convinced he became.

Mamie's legacy to him was more than a house.

She'd want her legacy to continue.

Now he had to convince one other person. Zoey Chavez.

"Zoey, you have company." Taffy Robbins, Zoey's close friend and occasional babysitter, stuck her pert face around the corner of the kitchen door. "Some guy in a blue pickup?"

Taffy's voice ended on a question. A photographer and sometimes writer for three area newspapers, Taffy was a hopeless romantic who swooned over old classic movies and music.

From the window over the kitchen sink where she filled a baby bottle with formula, Zoey peeked out at the shiny blue pickup truck parked next to the curb. Her breath caught.

He was still in Rosemary Ridge.

With a mixture of relief and irritation, she groused, "John-Parker Wisdom."

"Oh. Is he the guy that your aunt—"

Zoey interrupted before Taffy could rehash the painful truth. "Yes. That's him."

Taffy pulled a face, a black ponytail on either side of her head swaying. "And here I thought you had a new man in your life you weren't telling me about. Is he cute at all?"

Zoey glared at her friend. Taffy knew the last thing on

Zoey's mind was romance. With anyone. Her late husband had burned all the romance right out of her.

However, as much as she didn't *want* to see John-Parker again, she had to. He held her future in his untrustworthy hands.

Two days had passed since their confrontation at the lawyer's office and she'd started to worry he'd left town. Again. Leaving her homeless. Again.

She was still coming to terms with Mamie's will. She'd blamed John-Parker, which she knew wasn't fair. But she couldn't bring herself to blame Mamie. She'd loved her too much, and Mamie must have thought she was doing a good thing.

But what good could possibly come from such a bizarre arrangement?

"Want me to stick around as backup?" Taffy stepped all the way into the tired old kitchen and flexed a trim biceps.

Zoey snickered. Taffy was smaller than her and wouldn't hurt a flea. "I don't think he's dangerous."

"You said he was a security specialist, right?" Taffy tiptoed up to stare out at the truck.

"Right."

"Those guys are muscled to the max and always packing heat."

Zoey snorted. "Like you've known so many security specialists. And 'packing heat'? Really? Are you watching gangster movies these days?"

"Hey!" Taffy pretended hurt. "I work for the newspaper. I know stuff."

She did. That was a fact. "If John-Parker eliminates me, he loses everything, so I think I'm safe."

"Good to know."

They watched as the tall man exited the truck.

Zoey couldn't take her eyes off him. But not because he looked fit and lean in casual jeans, gleaming boots and a pristinely white button-down shirt. She needed to know who

John-Parker Wisdom had become after he'd left Mamie's home. What kind of man was she being forced to deal with? Mamie hadn't spoken to him in fifteen years. Why had she trusted him to make the right decisions? And why had she pitted the two of them against each other?

He circled the front of his truck, carrying a pair of bags. Gift bags.

Zoey frowned. "What is he doing?"

Taffy bounced up and down, patting her hands together like an excited kid. "Oooh, presents."

"Taffy, stop!"

The unrepentant photographer shrugged. "Sorry. Time for me to leave." In imitation of a traditional phone receiver, she put a finger and thumb up to her cheek. "Call me. I want a full report."

"I will."

As her friend disappeared out the front door, most certainly to stop John-Parker for a brief interrogation, Zoey capped the baby bottle and then followed the sound of a knock to the front door. Olivia, at eight months, spotted the bottle in Zoey's hand and abandoned her messy game of emptying every toy from a basket in pursuit of her mother. The kid could crawl faster than her three-year-old brother could walk.

Handing the baby the bottle and scooping her onto a hip, Zoey opened the front door.

If her belly did an uncharacteristic swoop, the cause was low blood sugar, not the semi-handsome man on her porch. At breakfast, she hadn't eaten anything except a banana and a bite of Owen's leftover toast.

Lifting a hand, she waved at Taffy as she hopped into her retro VW Bug. The one with a sunflower painted on the hood.

"Friend of yours?" John-Parker Wisdom offered her a gift bag.

"Yes." *None of your business.*

"Inquisitive, isn't she?"

Zoey snorted and eyed the gift bag with suspicion. "What's this?"

The tiny lines around his eyes crinkled. He had pretty eyes with exactly the right number of dark eyelashes to be noticeable while still being manly. And something she hadn't expected… A twinkle. The man's eyes twinkled.

"Not a snake, I promise."

Pretty eyes or not, she wouldn't put it past him. He could hand her a poisonous viper and have clear sailing toward Mamie's estate.

Except, he wouldn't inherit anything, and she wasn't being very nice.

She still didn't take the bag.

About that time, Owen arrived to cling to her skirt and peek around at the visitor.

"Hi."

The nemesis on the porch went to a crouch in front of her son, setting the two bags aside. "Hi, Owen. Remember me? I'm John-Parker. Will your mommy let me come in? I have a present for you."

Oh, he did not play fair.

Owen eased out from behind her and approached the man with more boldness than usual.

Presents had that effect on children.

With a huff to show her excess irritation with his manipulative ploys, she said, "You might as well. We have to talk anyway."

John-Parker rose, but to her surprise, he lifted Owen up with him.

Something inside her softened, though only momentarily. Sweet, innocent Owen didn't know this man wanted to steal his only hope of a better life.

There was, however, a certain appeal about a man with a child in his arms. Noticeably muscular arms. And shoulders.

Whatever his security business entailed, he did not sit behind a desk all day.

*Focus, Zoey. This is life and death. Kind of.* Life anyway. Hers. And the kids.

She led them into the living room, acutely aware of the tall man at her side. Was that Irish Spring soap she smelled? "Might as well sit down."

With a wry quirk of lips, he said, "I'll pass on the couch. Which, for the record, has got to go."

On principle, she wanted to disagree but couldn't. The couch was beyond help, but with an ancient hide-a-bed inside, it weighed a ton. She couldn't budge the monstrosity. "There are other chairs."

"Owen and I will take the floor for now. Right, Owen?"

Agreeable lamb that he was, Owen grinned. "Yep. You gots presents."

"For your sister, too."

Defeated, Zoey added Olivia and her bottle to the faded area rug and then joined them, glad she'd vacuumed last night after the babies were in bed. With both Owen and Olivia spending more time on the floor than anywhere else, she worked overtime to keep it clean.

Would John-Parker even notice that she tried her best to care for Mamie's home? Would he criticize the run-down, neglected areas? She'd been too financially strained to pay for repairs or new furniture, but she wasn't lazy. She could clean. Besides, the attorney had told her to do nothing until June first. Or until this man was found.

A squeal of delight ripped from her son. With the help of the man threatening his future, Owen, in a flurry of white tissue paper, pulled a toy dump truck loaded with plastic balls from the bag.

"A twuck. A twuck, Mommy." He held it up.

"I see that."

Her eyes met John-Parker's. *Briber*, she telegraphed with lowered eyebrows and pursed lips.

John-Parker smiled. Then he winked. Of all things! The

man had the audacity to wink as if he knew exactly what he was up to.

"Want me to show you how it works?" he asked Owen.

Obediently, her precious boy handed over the prized toy.

John-Parker ripped off the plastic surrounding the dump bed.

"See this button?" He took Owen's tiny hand in his much larger one and showed him how to press the release. The bed of the truck popped up, spilling out the colorful balls.

Owen chortled. "I do it."

John-Parker closed the dump bed, helped Owen reload the balls, and watched with an oddly tender smile as the child pushed the lever, spilling the balls all over again.

By now, Olivia had finished her bottle and crawled toward the action, though she was more interested in the tissue paper the two males had tossed aside.

Zoey scooted closer, too, not to be near John-Parker, though he'd definitely won a brownie point with the dump truck, but to stop Olivia from eating the tissue. Everything went in that child's mouth.

John-Parker pushed the remaining gift bag toward Zoey. "Yours and the baby's are in this bag."

"*Mine?* Why?" Now, she was really suspicious. Why was he, who'd accused of her fraudulently getting Aunt Mamie to agree to the will, suddenly giving her gifts? A Trojan horse perhaps?

"Peace offering?" His brow furrowed with the question.

Peace? With him?

Was there any other way to get where she needed to be?

Not quite ready to give in, she said, "We'll see."

The baby's toy was on top. A musical plush puppy with light-up buttons on the feet, hands, ears and heart.

"These are nice, John-Parker. Thank you." If she sounded flat, her emotion was consternation not ingratitude.

What was she going to do about this guy? If he left, she was ruined. If he stayed, no telling what he'd want to do with

Aunt Mamie's property. Already, he lobbied for the upper hand and, for the sake of her babies, she couldn't allow that.

"I wasn't sure what to get," he said. "I don't know much about kids, but Google and a nice lady at the store helped me out. I wasn't sure of the kids ages so if these are wrong—"

"They're perfect." There. More grateful-sounding.

"You haven't looked at yours."

Zoey didn't want to. She was afraid if she did, she'd fall for what was obviously a buttering-up-for-the-kill ploy. A decision to leave. Or worse, to stay and renovate the house into a bowling alley or something.

She really couldn't take any more bad news.

Fumbling with the bag, hesitant to look inside, she glanced up and caught those pretty gray eyes quietly watching her with an expression that made her wonder if he was uncertain. Vulnerable even. As if he cared that she liked whatever he'd chosen.

"I suppose you're going to stare at me until I look."

A tiny smile lifted the corners of his mouth. "I am."

With a sigh that was more pretend than aggravation, she reached inside the bag and retrieved a square box. A soft rattling sound came from inside.

She hiked an eyebrow at him. "Sounds like a rattlesnake to me."

He barked a short laugh. "Be brave. Open it."

Challenged now, and curious, though she hadn't intended to be, she removed the lid, folded away the tissue and lifted out a uniquely beautiful, stunningly perfect wind chime. From a teal dragonfly dangled small translucent sea glass in iridescent shades of blue and green. As she held up the chime, the glass emitted a gentle, pleasant tinkle, a whisper of ocean and sunshine.

"How did you know?" The words slipped out with the hint of wonder and pleasure that she felt.

"Know what?"

"That I love dragonflies. And wind chimes."

He shrugged, though she could see he was pleased. "I noticed your bracelet in the lawyer's office, and everyone likes wind chimes, don't they?"

She'd worn the dragonfly bracelet that day; a Christmas gift from Mamie. "I do. So did Mamie."

A pain she didn't want to acknowledge pinched behind his eyes. "I know. The dragonfly is LED. He lights up at night."

"Maybe she's a she."

"To be that pretty, yeah, probably."

Okay. She hadn't expected agreement. A battle-of-the-sexes argument perhaps but not an almost-compliment.

She didn't quite know what to make of John-Parker Wisdom. Today he was a courteous, even thoughtful gentleman, kind to her children, smiling and generous. At Buckner and Buckner, he'd been an angry, accusing menace. She could not allow herself to forget for one minute how he'd abandoned Aunt Mamie.

She felt off-balance. Unsure. Scared.

Finally, she pushed up from the floor. "I'll hang the chimes on the back porch out of the wind."

"Right. The wind. I'd forgotten how wild the wind could be in Oklahoma."

She wondered what else he had forgotten in fifteen years. More than that, she wondered what today would bring. Would her family become homeless? Or would John-Parker agree to her plans for the house?

When he unraveled his long legs and stood, she had a feeling she was about to find out.

# *Chapter Five*

John-Parker had planned this meeting as precisely as possible, including as many variables as he could imagine. This was the way he planned his security details. It was the way he planned his life. And now, he'd plan this renovation of Miss Mamie's home the same way.

Zoey Chavez was one of his unknown variables. He liked to neutralize as many unknowns as possible when stepping into a new situation. This one was no different.

He hoped the gifts had softened her up, though he was smart enough to know she was far from being neutral about him or their situation. At least, she wasn't yelling that he was worthless scum who deserved nothing. He already knew that. He'd battled this painful truth, come to a decision, and decided to forge onward in an effort to do what Mamie would have wanted. And perhaps to find redemption in the doing. *That* part he was sure of. Zoey, not so much.

"I assume you came to discuss the inheritance."

"Yes," he said. "Calmly. Respectfully."

"Are you offering or warning?"

"Both. No hysterics from either of us. A respectful, adult discourse with all the options and individual desires on the table. Neither expected this to happen, so let's be rational as we work things out. No shouts or accusations."

She sucked in a breath and, for a moment, he thought she'd taken his words as insult.

Then she breathed out and nodded. "All right. Agreed. Would you like some tea? Or water?"

"Miss Mamie's sweet tea?" He'd not had a satisfactory glass of Southern sweet tea since leaving Rosemary Ridge. Mamie had made the best.

"One and the same. She taught me."

"A glass sounds good." He followed her to the kitchen door. "Will the tots be okay alone?"

"I can watch them from the table if you'd prefer to sit in here." She motioned to the long, scarred table that adorned one side of the old-fashioned kitchen. The eat-in style was popular once more, but this kitchen was not even close to modern. He planned to change that. Open concept was the way to go. Knock out a wall here and there, open things up, add another bathroom.

Still, nostalgia flooded him as he settled at one side of the table, leaving the view to the living room wide open for Zoey.

Maybe he'd keep this old table, scars and all. A symbol. A memory. He could almost see his foster brothers gathered around and hear Miss Mamie's voice as she prayed over the meal or they battled through mountains of homework. They'd solved a lot of problems around this old table.

After placing two amber-colored glasses near his elbow, Zoey grabbed a notebook and pen from a drawer and took the chair to his left at the end.

"What did you decide?"

He hiked his eyebrows. "So, cut to the chase? No pleasantries?"

"We already did that." She tossed a long strand of dark hair over one slender shoulder. She had thick hair, glossy, wavy, the kind a man liked to touch. Some men. Not him. Certainly not hers. She'd probably bite his hand.

"Presents are a nice touch," she went on, "but they won't feed my children. We might as well get this discussion over with. Three months go fast."

She doubted him. Not that he could blame her. Mamie, apparently, never had, no matter how miserably he'd failed her.

He took a sip of the sweet tea and murmured his approval. He had to give Zoey credit, at least about the tea. She had captured the essence of his foster mother's brew.

Rubbing damp hands together, he caught the worry in her gaze and asked, "What will you do if I forfeit my share?"

She blinked in surprise. "You're still in town, so I thought—"

"Answer the question, please." He needed to know. The right answer could confirm what he believed the Lord was leading him to do.

She bristled. "I won't be interrogated."

Okay. He'd come on too strong.

He held out a hand in apology. "Sorry. That wasn't my meaning."

"What *did* you mean?

He sighed. The woman was about as difficult as an angry badger. So much for respectful and calm.

"Zoey, you have two kids. What will you do if this house and whatever money Mamie left you reverts to a trust and you have to move elsewhere? Do you have the needed funds?"

"That's not your business, Mr. Wisdom."

"As little as you think of me, I don't feel right about leaving you with nothing."

Her shoulders drooped a little. "So, you are forfeiting? Walking away, leaving Mamie's inheritance as if it's nothing."

He flinched. She didn't know him. Couldn't know he'd do anything for Mamie Bezek. Naturally, she expected the worst.

"Before I can answer your question, I'd like an answer to mine. What's your plan if I head back to Arizona tomorrow?"

"Try to find a better job, a cheap rental and a good daycare." She hitched that small proud chin of hers. "I'll survive. We'll survive."

She was strong and courageous, but John-Parker was an expert in reading people. Zoey Chavez was scared.

The thought that John-Parker would drive away and leave her penniless scared Zoey to pieces. She hated that. Hated being dependent on his good graces for anything. Hated being dependent on any man after Vic had taught her the danger of such dependence.

Longing for a home and family of her own, she'd married Vic Chavez believing he was her knight in shining armor. But after Owen came along, their relationship fizzled. According to her husband, she spent too much time with the baby. She didn't pay enough attention to her man. It was her fault he lost his temper. But he promised to do better if she would.

So she worked harder to make him happy, wanting to believe he loved her.

That is, until Vic died along with his lover and she'd become a homeless widow with a baby on one hip, pregnant with another, and no one to turn to.

After the way John-Parker had hurt Mamie, she certainly didn't trust him. She wanted to hate him.

But, for some reason, Mamie had loved him. She'd confided as much to Zoey at the very end when he still hadn't been found or come back to visit. She'd loved the boy John-Parker, though she'd never revealed why he'd meant more than any of the others.

Instead of dwelling on the worry that she'd be left high and dry without him, Zoey got straight to the point. Her goal. Her dream. "I have a plan for the house."

"So do I." Caution sprang up around him. A quiet tension. "Let's hear yours first."

Easy so far. At least he was listening.

"I'd like to renovate and bring everything up to today's standards for a very nice family home, then put the property on the market. I've looked at a few comparable homes in Rosemary Ridge and I think we can get top dollar if we invest the available funds Mr. Buckner mentioned. Once we sell, we can split a significant profit."

"Then take the money and go our separate ways? Is that it?"

Since he put it like that. "That seems the sensible thing to do, don't you think? I mean, what else is there to do except to sell? We can't cut a house down the middle and each take a half. If we sell, you'll have your share, I'll have mine, and you can go back to Phoenix better off than you arrived. If the will allowed us to sell now, I'd do that, but according to Mr. Buckner, we have to use the three months to renovate. If we do a good job, we can sell for a nice profit."

She hoped she didn't sound mercenary. She was being pragmatic. A benefit for both of them. Surely, he could see that.

Mamie wanted them both to benefit as much as possible. Right?

John-Parker sat quietly, contemplative for several long moments, eyebrows pulled together in a slight furrow that emphasized the two-lane scar. Her gaze settled on that scar, curious, hopeful, nervous.

The ticktock of her heart seemed to grow louder in the silence.

Dragging her gaze to the living room, she checked on the little ones. Owen patiently showed Olivia how to place colorful shapes into a matching hole and patted her back as he guided her to the correct placement. Her boy, so smart and gentle.

A swell of love increased her anxiety. Her babies deserved better than she'd been able to give them. Now, Mamie was giving her an opportunity to make a better life for all of them. Even for John-Parker, if he could agree to staying in Rosemary Ridge until the house was repaired and sold.

Lips pressed together, Zoey glanced down at the doodles on the notebook. Doodles she'd done dozens of times in planning the renovations she wanted for Aunt Mamie's house. She needed John-Parker because she needed that money, but she would not beg or grovel ever again. Reason, argue, fight, yes. Grovel, never.

John-Parker sipped from the half-empty glass and set it carefully aside.

"I can't do that. I won't agree to sell Mamie's house."

Her hopes plummeted. He was forfeiting? "So, you'll walk away from what could be a significant inheritance?"

"I can't do that either."

"You're not making sense. Are you staying for the terms of the will or not?" And if he was, what else could they do but sell and divide the money?

He sighed, long and hard, his broad shoulders lifting, cheeks expanding in a gust of air. "I visited Mamie's grave. Then I made a phone call to Brandt James, my business partner in Phoenix, and another to Buckner and Buckner. Good counsel, like the Bible says to ask for."

And he'd gone shopping for presents, too. "You've been busy."

"After much prayer and discussion, I know what Mamie would want and that's what I intend to do."

Nerves tingled along Zoey's spine.

She had a feeling she was not going to like his plan.

"Miss Mamie lived her life to help people. Teenage boys. The ones no one else wanted. Boys like me."

John-Parker leaned both forearms on the table, fingers lightly laced to present a calm façade, though his pulse ticked away on the inside of his neck.

Panic caused irrational behavior. Fear froze the thought processes. John-Parker Wisdom never panicked and refused to be afraid.

Zoey sat straighter, watching him as if he were the rattlesnake she'd accused him of bringing to her.

He was good at reading body language, and hers was wary, anxious, eager to see him gone. *After* they sold the house.

Which was not going to happen.

If she had one bit of sympathy for him or the other lost boys, she didn't show it. But he didn't care what she thought. Abandoned boys, troubled boys, were worth fighting for. He and Brandt were living proof.

"I strongly believe Miss Mamie would want her legacy

to continue. I propose a complete renovation of the home, starting immediately."

"Good. My thoughts exactly. Renovate and sell."

"Wait." He held up a hand. "Hear me out."

She dipped her head in acquiescence. "Go ahead. But I like the renovation part, which means you're not giving Mamie's property to a trust."

She wouldn't like this part.

"Look, Zoey, Mamie made a difference here. She saved lives. Mine, Brandt's, others."

"Mine and my children's. She did some wonderful things for the people in this house."

He pointed both index fingers at her. "So, you get it. You understand why her legacy must continue. We'll turn this property into a bigger, better, fully modernized home, and maybe even a training center, but a real home for teenage foster boys who no one else will take."

Alarm widened her eyes. Zoey jerked to a stand. The flowers on her dress vibrated with tension. "No. We have to sell."

John-Parker tried to keep the distaste from showing on his face. So, he'd been correct. Zoey only cared about the money.

"Mamie would want this house to go on serving others," he said with a calm stubbornness. "I won't sell."

So, they were at an impasse.

If she wanted a fight, she'd get one. And he would win.

Zoey Chavez cared nothing about Mamie's wishes. She didn't even care that this house had nurtured so many young men, as well as herself. Money was her focus, her goal.

Zoey huffed and crossed her arms. "How would you know what she'd want? You haven't spoken to her in fifteen years."

A guilty throb started up in his temple. He'd deserved that comment. He hated her derision, but he'd earned it. She apparently thought as little of him as he thought of her.

"Look," he said. "I've decided to reside in Rosemary Ridge for the terms of the will. Fortunately, my work allows that. Let's start there. I'm not leaving you high and dry."

She sniffed, her upper lip curled. “Should I say thank you?”

Her tone made it clear that she wouldn’t, so he skipped right past the snarky comment. “The house needs major renovations. We agreed on that already, right?”

“Absolutely.”

“Good. Then let’s both make a list of the things we think are important, including our visions for the property.” Maybe they could find a middle ground, or better yet, she’d see the value in his plan and abandon hers.

Sell Mamie’s house? No way. She’d either agree to honor Miss Mamie or, if she was a gold-digger, as he suspected, he’d fight her in court if he had to.

“We’ll do whatever work we can ourselves, but I’ll start asking around town about contractors for the rest.”

“Fair enough. I can check material and furnishing prices and make a list of those. I’ll also call Mr. Buckner about the budget.”

He allowed a wry chuckle. “Well, look at the two of us, agreeing on not one but three things.”

She laid the pen aside with a resolute snap. “I’ll make your lists and listen to your ideas, Mr. Wisdom, but I won’t change my mind about selling this house.”

John-Parker’s jaw tightened.

He’d see about that.

Zoey had dreaded this moment for three months. The day she started boxing up Aunt Mamie’s belongings. That project was one other thing she and John-Parker had agreed upon. The house had to be cleared out before they could demo and renovate.

Mamie’s personal space would be the hardest. Zoey decided to start there and get the most painful part over with.

She plopped Olivia and Owen each into a cardboard carton and started to drag them toward Mamie’s living quarters at the back of the house. Two birds with one stone. Take the kids and the packing boxes at the same time.

She patted Olivia's tiny hands. "Hold on, baby."

A knock sounded at the door.

"I get it, Mom." Owen climbed out of his box and raced on green-dinosaur tennis shoes toward the front door.

"Wait. Don't open that."

Her boy skidded to a stop. "It's the nice man. The presents man."

"Oh. Right." She'd known he'd arrive at some point this morning, whether she wanted him there or not.

Blowing a loose hair off her forehead, Zoey clicked the lock.

Before she could offer further warning to her son about never opening the door without her present, Owen launched himself against John-Parker's legs. "Want to play cars?"

John-Parker patted her son's T-shirt-clad back. "Sure. First, though, your mommy and I have some work to do. Okay?"

"Uh-huh." His little face lifted up and up toward John-Parker. "You can drive me to Mom's work."

John-Parker tilted his head at Zoey in question.

"The boxes are his cars today. The easiest way to take packing boxes and two kids to the back of the house is to 'drive' the kids to work in the boxes."

"Smart."

If he knew how stupid she'd been in her life, he wouldn't say such a thing. Nevertheless, the compliment rode easy on her shoulders. She hadn't had many of those until she'd come to live with Mamie.

Interesting that this stranger she wanted to dislike offered a compliment she'd never heard from her late husband.

She tossed her hair back, feeling a bit sassy. Not flirty. Certainly not *that*. "That's me. Smart Zoey. A genius, really, full of brilliant ideas."

He grinned.

She grinned back. A butterfly fluttered in her chest. Silly thing. She wasn't attracted to John-Parker, she was being practical. They'd been forced to work together for the next few months. Might as well be as cordial as possible.

Even if she'd never forgive him for ignoring Aunt Mamie.

All thoughts of attraction disappeared along with her smile. *No grinning. No flirting. Stick to the agenda.*

Owen hopped back into his cardboard "car," his brown eyes locked on the tall man. "Mom drives Livia. You drive me. Okay?"

"You got it, little buddy." To her, he said, "Where to?"

"Mamie's room."

Some of his jaunty attitude fell away. "Already?"

"Might as well get it over with."

His stormy eyes stared at her for what seemed an eternity, something—*something*—in his expression she didn't understand, before turning his attention to Owen.

"Ready, Owen?"

"Yep." Her son gripped small fingers on either side of the box. "Go fast."

They took off, leaving the girls behind. Raucous race car sounds, provided unexpectedly by the adult driver, trailed behind them.

"*Vroom, vroom, vroom. Errr, errr.* There's a corner ahead. Hold on tight." John-Parker glanced back, saw her trailing along with Olivia. Slowly. "They're gaining on us, Owen, my man. Gotta speed up."

More sound effects.

Owen's laughter filled the house.

And her heart.

She was determined not to like John-Parker Wisdom. Cordial, yes. Friendly, no. Why did he have to be nice to her kids?

Was it to soften her up so she'd agree to his outlandish plan?

Or was he a genuinely kind man?

The jury, as they say, was still out.

# *Chapter Six*

He wished Zoey would smile occasionally. Her suspicious glares, aimed in his direction, made him feel like a convicted ax murderer.

The wayward thought shot through John-Parker's head while he was in mid-motor sound, whipping the cardboard box around corners and listening to Owen's giggle. The kid was cute. Sweet, too. Some of his friends in Phoenix had kids, but he'd never paid them much attention.

Something about Owen touched him. Maybe because the boy didn't have a dad. John-Parker understood that well.

As he approached the suite at the back of the house, reluctance filled him. Packing away Mamie's personal effects would not be easy for him, but apparently Zoey felt differently. She had used the phrase, "Get it over with." Was she really that coldhearted?

The door was open, so he pushed the boxful of boy inside, spun him around a couple of times for good measure, and smiled at the childish delight.

When they came to a rest, Zoey and the pretty baby girl watched them from the doorway.

"Mom, Mom." Owen catapulted out of the box. "I'm Mario."

Zoey hiked an eyebrow toward John-Parker.

"Mario Andretti, greatest race car driver ever."

"Yep. That's me." Owen patted the T-Rex on the front of his shirt.

"I see. Well, Mario—" she lifted Olivia to the floor "—you and Olivia play cars while John-Parker and Mommy fill these boxes."

"I can help," the boy said hopefully.

She bent for a quick hug. "Not this time, bud."

Seeing the disappointment on the boy's face, John-Parker interrupted. "When I pack up the den, I could use a helper. Do you know one?"

"Me." Owen straightened proudly. "I help you."

John-Parker stuck out a hand. "Deal. You and me and the den, little man."

As he closed his much larger fingers around the boy's tiny hand, something warm and tender pushed inside his chest.

Being in this house, in Mamie's suite, was getting to him.

He turned his attention to the room, caught Zoey's mouthed *Thank you,* and shrugged. He hadn't made the offer for her. He'd done it for the child.

And it felt good. Tender feelings weren't his usual emotion and he was surprised a kid had stirred them so easily.

"Let's get to work."

With a nod, she opened a dresser drawer.

The dread in John-Parker's chest turned to near panic. A memory pushed in of another time when he'd searched through Mamie's belongings. A time of selfishness, of thievery. Though God had forgiven him, he'd never know if Mamie had. He certainly hadn't forgiven himself.

"Uh—no," he said. "No. Stop."

She paused, one hand inside the clothing drawer, expression quizzical.

"Look, Zoey. I, uh… This is too personal." He pinched his lip, fighting emotions he didn't want to feel. "Riffling through her clothing feels wrong, an invasion of privacy."

As if she understood, which wasn't possible, Zoey removed her hand and closed the drawer. "I'll do this part later. We don't have to start with her clothing."

John-Parker breathed an inward sigh of relief. "Right. Good. We can hire someone."

Zoey's back stiffened, clearly affronted. "Never will I allow a stranger to sort through Aunt Mamie's belongings. The clothes remind me of how much I owe her."

"Okay. Okay. But I'm a man. I have no business pawing

through Mamie's dresser. No one does." He sounded like an embarrassed schoolboy.

"Who do you think bathed and dressed her in her final weeks, John-Parker? Who do you think washed these items and put them in these drawers?"

The comment was a stab to the chest. Mamie hadn't been able to care for herself. She, who had cared for the whole world, had been helpless—except for this woman in the colorful sundress. The woman he believed to be a gold-digger.

He hadn't made a solid evaluation about Zoey Chavez, and he was not one to let down his guard, but maybe she wasn't as bad as he thought. She'd been here. He had not.

He could not erase the thought that he'd failed the one person in the world who'd cared about him.

Failure. Guilt. A grief too big to ignore.

The only way to redemption was through keeping her memory alive with this house.

"I'll pack her books." He tugged a box toward the wall of shelves. "You can start on her closet."

As he began pulling items from a shelf, he said, "She loved books."

"Yes."

Packing her reading material was almost as painful as sorting through her clothing, although not as embarrassing.

"Classics." John-Parker rubbed a hand over a dusty volume of *To Kill a Mockingbird*. "She required each of us to read something from this shelf every month."

"Did you have a favorite?"

Sadly, he'd balked, arguing against using his brain for anything. He'd even pretended to read without seeing a word, but in the end, Mamie had not been fooled. She'd won and turned him into a lifetime reader by making him read aloud to her while she'd cooked dinner.

"*Huckleberry Finn*, maybe."

Zoey nodded. "I can see why you'd like that one."

"You can?"

One shoulder lifted. "A boy, unhappy with his lot in life, runs away to seek adventure."

He'd never considered the parallel. He'd simply admired Huck's courage. "I suppose so."

"Did you find it? The adventure?"

"More than I bargained for," he mused.

"Like Huck."

"I take it you've read Twain, too. Did she still have her weekly book club?"

"Oh, yes. No one lived in this house without reading and discussing books. Regularly."

He gave a short laugh. "She wouldn't own a TV. Claimed the programming stifled the imagination and intellect."

Books, puzzles, games like chess, science projects, even art had kept the rowdy bunch of boys busy, but no "idiot box," as she'd termed the TV.

"She hadn't changed her opinion. Boy, could she get on her soapbox about that issue."

John-Parker smiled, the memories unexpectedly sweet. Sometimes when he clicked on the big screen in his apartment, he wondered what Mamie would think. "She was unique."

"Yeah. Aunt Mamie was a very special woman."

Their gazes met and he saw the soft moisture gathered in Zoey's deep brown eyes. Tears glistened on her lashes.

Had he misjudged her? Maybe her feelings today while sorting through Mamie's personal effects were genuine. If they were, he'd have a harder time fighting her over this house. A much harder time.

Zoey's anger toward John-Parker slowly dissipated. His reaction to the clothing drawers had touched her heart, whether she wanted to admit it or not.

At first, as they'd cleared the room, conversation had been limited, stilted when it happened, but as she'd found items she wasn't sure what to do with and asked for his opinion, they'd both seemed to relax. The children, too, had provided a buffer. Owen latched onto John-Parker's attention every chance he got and she'd been impressed that the man hadn't left Olivia out of that attention.

"Do you have kids?" she asked after watching him replace a wheel on Owen's toy car.

"Me? No. Not married."

"Never?"

"Too busy. I travel a lot and my job is dangerous. Neither is conducive to romantic relationships."

"What exactly does a security specialist do?" She went to the walk-in closet and returned with yet another box to sort.

He told her about his job, but she could tell he left out the scary, dangerous parts. In fact, he sounded as if every assignment was a holiday with celebrities. Zoey doubted that, considering he'd already mentioned that his job was dangerous. That's why he wasn't married. Or at least part of the reason.

Still, she appreciated his conversational caution when her kids were in the room. No use spoiling their innocence with talk of terrorists, assassins and other evildoers. If that was the case.

"Do you like being a bodyguard?"

"Security specialist. I guard people, but we do more than that. We set up security in a way that mitigates trouble from the outset. We try to circumvent issues and people who pose a risk before anything bad can happen."

She barely understood what he was talking about. "How?"

He gave a short but impressive rundown of risk assessment, securing the venue, monitoring crowds, tight communication with other security, entrance-and-exit strategies.

Zoey's head began to spin. "I guess you are more than a bodyguard."

He chuckled and flexed an impressive biceps, clearly poking fun at himself. "Brawn over brains. That's me."

*Humble* was a word she wouldn't have used to describe John-Parker Wisdom, but after a litany of skills most people didn't have, he'd shrugged away a compliment.

Maybe there was more to him than met the eye.

To her consternation, what met the eye was impressive.

And that irritated her, to be honest. She had no intention of admiring this man. She had to work with him for three months, convince him to sell the remodeled house, and then she'd never have to see his impressive face again.

Ever.

More than a little aggravated at herself, Zoey turned her attention to a big box of Christmas gift wrap. The stuff she'd pulled out of Mamie's closet would fill a small store.

"Deciding what to do with all this is going to be a challenge," she muttered.

John-Parker held up a child's book that had lost the cover and some of the pages. The remaining pages were tattered, bent and smudged. "I wonder why she kept this? There aren't enough pages left to make a story."

"She wasn't one to toss out something if she had a use for it. Make-do Mamie."

"I heard her say that, too." He thumbed through the tattered pages, ending on the back cover. "Who was Brian?"

She shrugged. "She mentioned someone named Brian once, but that was toward the end when she was heavily medicated. I thought he must be a boy she'd fostered. When she'd dream, she'd murmur names sometimes." Including John-Parker's.

"Read this." He pushed the book toward her.

On her knees beside an overstuffed box of tattered garland, she leaned toward him and took the book.

"'To my beloved Brian. Happy 3rd birthday. With love, Mommy.'" Zoey looked up, bewildered. "The writing looks like Mamie's, but it couldn't be. She didn't have children."

"That we know of."

"I'm sure she didn't, John-Parker. If she'd had children, where are they? Where are their photos? With the way she loved people, Mamie would have had pictures hanging everywhere."

"True. This was probably a donated book. She got plenty of those over the years. Some were inscribed like this one."

"Mystery solved." She stood, hitched Olivia onto her side, and started toward the exit "I'm going for more packing boxes."

The Rosemary Ridge town council met on the final Monday of each month. Since he only had three months to make this dream a reality, and he'd already missed the May meeting, John-Parker wasted no time getting on the agenda for the end of June

In the weeks since his arrival, he'd filled out a mountain of paperwork for DCS, the Department of Children's Services, with more to come, including permits from the city to begin the remodel process.

He could handle those on his own.

Though he'd consulted an architect and general contractor for help with the plans, he preferred to do as much himself as possible. Thanks to Mamie and the military, he was reasonably handy. Forced to stay in Rosemary Ridge anyway, he needed to stay busy.

The more money he saved by doing the work himself, the more he could spend on improving the house and land. So, tonight he'd lay out his concept to the council and ask for their approval to pull work permits.

Knowing her opinion already, he hadn't mentioned this meeting to Zoey. He'd told her his plans for the house. She'd told him hers. He had to move forward.

Inside the 1930's rock building that housed city hall, John-Parker expected a light crowd. Rosemary Ridge wasn't big and most issues that came before a small-town council were simple. His certainly was.

Apparently, he'd been wrong. At least a dozen people jammed the small conference room and buzzed with conversation as if a council meeting was a neighborhood get-together at which someone promised to serve free barbecue.

Must be another issue on the agenda. Probably the rumble he'd read in the newspaper about losing the town's ambulance service. In fact, red-haired Clare Valandingham, with her notepad and variety of pens and pencils stuck in her curly hair, was here.

John-Parker checked his shiny boots for dirt one last time and hoped no one in the room recalled the street rat he'd once been. So far, as he'd shopped and obtained a temporary rental in town, no one had seemed unfriendly or pointed out his wayward teenage years, if they'd recognized his name at all.

Spotting a familiar pair of old-timers, he tapped the brim of his hat toward Wink and Frank Myrick. Wink waved him to an empty seat.

Removing the Stetson the way Miss Mamie would expect a gentleman to do, John-Parker nodded his way past a few familiar faces until he reached the chair.

"Howdy, John-Parker Wisdom," the diminutive cowboy said. "You're causing quite a stir."

"Me? How?" He placed the hat on his lap.

"This idea of yours to turn Mamie Bezek's house into a group home."

"She's always had a foster home there, so what's the problem?"

"Nah, Wink, people ain't here for that," Frank said. "It's the ambulance brouhaha stirring up folks. Look at all the old people in this room. They're scared they'll have a heart attack and no one will come get them to the hospital. Scared of dying, every one of them."

Frank didn't seem to be including himself in the "old" or "scared" category.

"Maybe," Wink replied, "but I heard Jessie Starks complaining about vandals and hoodlums at the coffee shop this morning when I was getting my latte."

Frank rolled his eyes. "Latte. Just plain coffee with milk, if you ask me, and he pays eight dollars for some teenager with a nose ring to pour it for him. It ain't even in a real cup. Pitiful."

John-Parker bit back a grin.

"That teenager is gainfully employed, which you would know nothing about, Frank Myrick. Now, I for one, think Johnny-Parker here has a fine notion and if Jane or her bunch fusses, I'm standing tall against her."

"You ain't never stood tall, brother." The old man guffawed.

"Thanks, Wink," John-Parker said. "I appreciate your support, but I don't expect a problem."

He was here for building permits. How problematic was a little paperwork?

"I reckon we're fixin' to find out." Frank motioned toward the front where Mayor Ben Jones called the meeting to order and the room quieted.

After the minutes were read and approved, Mayor Jones read the first items on the agenda, which were budget items, easily dispensed. Then came the topic of the ambulance service.

John-Parker noticed his name near the bottom. Zoey wouldn't be happy that he'd forged ahead without talking to her first, but time wasn't on his side. Even if she had some greedy notion of making big money off Mamie's house, John-Parker was convinced this was the right direction to take.

To the disgust of several senior citizens, only those with names listed on the agenda were allowed to speak, so the ambulance discussion was mercifully short. In the end, the council tabled the issue until more information and options for replacing the service were gathered.

Finally, John-Parker's request was read aloud by the mayor. "Seems a simple request to me. Anyone on the council have a comment or question for Mr. Wisdom about these permits?"

"I do." A gray-mustachioed council member, whose nameplate read Earl Beck, spoke up. "What exactly are you planning to do with this house, Mr. Wisdom? Why is an out-of-towner in charge of Mamie Bezek's home anyhow?"

"Now, Earl, that's not our business." The mayor looked

none too pleased that a council member had slowed the proceedings.

"But his purpose is. We live in this town. He doesn't. I heard he's planning to house a bunch of juvenile delinquents."

"Sir." John-Parker rose, keeping his outward cool but instantly hotter than a cheap phone. "That is not true. My plan is to keep Miss Mamie's legacy alive by providing a good home where boys can grow up to be solid citizens."

"Troubled boys." Earl clamped his lips tight.

"Rejected boys. Abandoned boys. Boys in need."

Another council member nodded. "As I recall, those boys caused some trouble."

Someone in the crowd murmured, "Plenty of it."

"Order," the mayor said.

John-Parker twisted the brim of his hat, reminding himself that a calm tone did more than anger. It was a lesson Mamie had tried to teach him and the military had pounded into him until he'd gotten the message. That cool demeanor in the face of difficulties made him a good security specialist.

Right now, he struggled not to lash out. Earl had poked a hot button inside him; a defensive place he'd thought was under control.

"I can't argue that a few things happened that shouldn't have. But this home aims to remediate those issues. Remember, if you will, that even boys from solid families sometimes get into trouble."

"That's true, Earl," the mayor said. "You know it, too, from personal experience."

Earl looked nonplussed, although his complexion reddened. "Don't matter. We ought not to borrow trouble. I thought when Mamie passed, we'd be done with hoodlums ruining the town."

A woman John-Parker recognized stood. "That house is in my neighborhood, Mayor, and I object."

"Jane, you're out of order."

With a huff, she regained her chair, talking all the way

down. "I still object. One of her street rats stole my daughter's bike."

Wink popped up out of his chair. "Jane, will you ever stop griping about that? It happened ten years ago. Your daughter doesn't even live at home anymore. Where she at now? Baltimore?"

The mayor rapped his gavel. "Sit down, Wink."

"I'm on the agenda, Mayor." Wink poked a finger at the mayor's desk. "Have a looky-see. Right there at the bottom, 'Wink Myrick, Esq.'"

John-Parker grinned at the old cowboy. He was a pistol, all right, and a good man to have on his side.

"I guess you are. Go ahead then, Wink. Have your say."

Wink sat down. "I'm done. For now."

The room chuckled. The mayor shook his head. "Then let's get on with this. I could be called out to a fire at any minute."

"Yeah," Earl griped, "started by some gangbanger this out-of-towner wants to put in Mamie's house."

John-Parker stood again, hat in his hand, and said, "I grew up here, sir. I'm not a stranger to this town."

"I know who you are. Don't think I've forgotten what you and your gang did."

"I've never been in a gang." To the mayor, he said, "If I may, Mr. Mayor, I'd like to address the council about my current situation."

Mayor Ben waved his gavel. "Go on. But if I get a call-out, we'll have to table this meeting for another time."

"Understood, sir. Thank you." Courtesy, Miss Mamie would say, won many a debate. "Currently, I own and operate a worldwide security agency out of Phoenix, Arizona. Silent Security. I'm a military veteran, a tax-paying citizen, and a Christian man who owes a great deal to Mamie Bezek. Yes, I made mistakes in my teen years and, as recompense, it's my sincerest desire to honor Miss Bezek's legacy of kindness and caring by keeping teenage foster boys, like myself and my current business partner were, off the streets. She changed our lives. I want to do the same for other young men in her memory."

"Is this a halfway house of some kind?" Beck asked. "A transition program for juvenile offenders, or what?"

"A home. Mamie's house will be a home, not a temporary shelter. A home with love and discipline where boys will learn values and character qualities they'll carry with them their entire lives. Hopefully, some job skills, too."

"You're saying every one of Mamie's foster kids made productive, law-abiding adults?" Earl's belligerent tone said he already knew the answer.

"I wouldn't know." Rio was probably in prison. Or dead. "Miss Mamie might not have saved us all, but she made a difference to me and my business partner. Don't other boys deserve the same shot? Don't you want this town to make a difference?"

"They made a difference in the past, and it wasn't a good one. My storage unit was broke into twice." Earl motioned to a man in the audience. "Hal didn't you have some vandalism at your place?"

"Yep. They stole some tools off my porch, too."

"Thieving rats. I won't have any more of them in my neighborhood."

"Sit down, Jane. You're out of order. Again."

Jane obviously didn't care what the mayor said. "Ben, you know we're right. We can't allow this to happen again."

"Order, Jane, before I ask Deputy Simpkins to remove you."

"Well." She huffed loudly and sat, arms crossed, glare toward John-Parker enough to start that fire the mayor worried about.

He hadn't expected this kind of reaction. Hostility, anger, resistance, and hearing the term "thieving rats" stung like a venomous wasp. All he wanted was a few building permits.

Wink popped up again. "Earl, did any of you prove Mamie's boys guilty of those crimes?"

"No, but we knew. The police chief was soft on them 'cause he and Mamie Bezek went to the same church. Now that we have a new leader in the police department and Mamie's trouble-makers are gone, crime is down."

"Don't mean that her boys were responsible. I move that we approve Mr. Wisdom's requests."

"You're not on the council, Wink," the mayor said, clearly beleaguered by the unexpected discussion.

"Then one of you needs to get busy and do the job we elected you to do."

Mayor Jones looked upward and shook his head before saying, "Everybody calm down and let's think about this rationally. All Mr. Wisdom is requesting are building permits to remodel an old, run-down house. We have safety and nuisance ordinances in Rosemary Ridge that dictate, among other things, that a property must be kept in good repair, which he desires to do. Is that right, Mr. Wisdom?"

"Yes, Mayor."

"That's not all he wants to do." Earl tapped a pen against the stack of papers in front of him. "I say we invoke the nuisance ordinance you just mentioned and nip this delinquent problem before it starts up again."

"Let's avoid that by giving him the building permits."

"That's not the part of the ordinance I'm talking about, Ben. Remember when those homesteaders put eight hogs in their backyard, over by the grade school? The nuisance ordinance saved the whole neighborhood from being uprooted."

"We're discussing people, not hogs, Earl."

"The purpose of the ordinance is to protect the neighborhood, whether hogs, people, or overgrown lawns."

The mayor looked to a forty-something brunette taking notes. "Does the nuisance ordinance apply in this case, Maggie?"

"Well, let me look a minute." She opened the cell phone at her elbow, typed in something, and scrolled. "Here it is. According to City Ordinance 91, paragraph one, a nuisance occurs when one property owner uses their property in a way that prevents other neighboring owners from enjoying their property."

Earl gave a loud huff of victory. "There you go. Those boys were a nuisance, ruining the neighborhood. Folks like Jane certainly couldn't enjoy their property with Mamie's boys running loose, stealing, playing loud music, and raising all kinds of Cain. Isn't that right, Jane?"

"Absolutely. We feared for our lives."

John-Parker would have rolled his eyes if the matter had been less serious. He couldn't quite believe this was happening.

Wink popped up like an overwound jack-in-the-box. "Mayor, you can't invoke the nuisance clause in this case. It's not legal."

The mayor held up a stop-sign hand. "You may be right, Wink. We'll need input from the city attorney before any decision is made."

John-Parker felt his hopes slipping away. Time was of the essence. To him, anyway.

"Since the main sticking point appears to be the use of the property following the remodel, I propose this," the mayor continued. "Approve the building permits and table the nuisance decision. We need more time to think and study the situation."

Ordinances? Attorneys? John-Parker closed his eyes for a quick regroup.

*Lord, what's happening here?*

He'd been certain he was doing the right thing. Now what?

"We might as well vote," one of the council members said, "I move we approve the building permits but table any efforts to turn the house into a juvenile home."

"The motion has been made." Mayor Jones gazed around at his other three council members. "Do I hear a second?"

Earl Beck crossed his arms, jaw set tighter than a bulldog's.

"I'll second," Maggie said.

"All in favor of the motion as stated, raise your right hand."

All but Earl's hand went up.

"Finally." Mayor Ben slammed his gavel. Maggie jumped. "Mr. Wisdom, you can remodel. We'll revisit the rest at a future meeting."

Jane blurted, "Don't tell him that."

The mayor looked to the ceiling and shook his head in despair. Jane, apparently, had no intention of keeping quiet, regardless of *Roberts' Rules of Order.*

Dismayed, John-Parker thanked the mayor and regained his seat. The next council meeting was at the very end of July, only a month before he and Zoey had to give Lonnie Buckner their decision. He didn't have time to wait.

He stared at his hat, pondering his next move. How could he make this work? Was he even supposed to? Or should he give in to Zoey's plans to sell and simply ride out the next few months until he could leave this town and never look back?

He couldn't. For Mamie's sake. And his own hounding conscience.

Frank clapped a large hand on his shoulder. "Don't worry, son. We'll do some research and talk to the city attorney about this whole deal. We got pull."

The old gents meant well, but John-Parker's hope for redemption had fallen to the floor and floundered. He could remodel the way Zoey wanted, but he couldn't move forward with every item needed for a group foster home until at least next month. Nor would DCS approve his paperwork without the city's approval of that home.

All he could do for now was forge ahead with the basic remodel and pray that something changed. Fast.

# *Chapter Seven*

"I heard what you did."

The next morning, Zoey met her nemesis at the front door, ready to pounce. The underhanded, double-dealing, overconfident excuse for a human had tried to advance his own agenda without consulting her.

Not happening. Never again would she allow a man to direct her path. She'd barely slept last night she'd been so upset.

"Yeah? What did you hear?" John-Parker stepped into the house, toting a stack of plastic storage tubs that smelled like cinnamon and acting as innocent as her baby daughter.

Well, he did not fool her. Not one bit.

"Last night's town council meeting. You tried to sabotage my plans for Aunt Mamie's house."

Tried and failed, to her delight, but still, he should not have gone behind her back. No doubt, he'd try again. And again. She didn't trust him as far as she could throw a school bus.

Thank goodness for nosy neighbors. Jane Renfroe, from four houses down, telephoned late last night to warn her that some out-of-town guy wanted to turn her home into a halfway house for teenage delinquents. Jane was as furious as Zoey, which was great news. If the neighbors were on her side, she'd win.

"Sabotage is a strong word, but if you heard about the meeting, you also know I failed to secure their full approval. We have the building permits but only to renovate as a regular family residence."

"Jane told me." That, at least, had been a relief.

"We had to acquire building permits, Zoey, no matter what we do with the house. I applied as required by law. The council asked for details. I gave them. I had no idea I'd come under attack because of a routine request."

Zoey frowned. "They attacked you personally?"

Was that why he looked tired and sad this morning? Or was he upset because he'd lost, she'd won, and he was stuck in Rosemary Ridge for three months to make her dreams come true?

Except he wasn't stuck. If his foster home idea was out of the running, he could drive away in his big blue truck and never look back. And she'd be the one who was stuck.

"Let's just say I took strong offense at terms like 'street rats' and 'gangsters,' and foster kids being lumped into the same category as rooting hogs."

Zoey gasped. "They said those things?"

He gave a tired shrug, so she knew they had.

If she wasn't trying to protect her own future, she'd feel sorry for John-Parker. He didn't deserve that kind of treatment. No one did.

"People have strong opinions, Zoey. Let's forget about last night for now and discuss doughnuts." He reached inside one of the plastic tubs and then handed her a white bakery box. "Will you make coffee to go with those?"

During last night's phone call, nosy neighbor Jane had "warned" Zoey about the problem John-Parker and "his kind" would cause, but she'd failed to mention a direct attack on the man's character during the meeting. Even though Zoey didn't trust him, John-Parker wasn't evil. Conniving maybe, but not wicked.

She received the white box, the smell of fresh pastries and cinnamon rising to her nose. "That's all you have to say about what happened last night?"

"Yes."

Her ruffled feathers weren't soothed at all. The trouble was, she didn't know if she was more upset with him or with whomever had said mean things to him. Being a foster kid had not been his doing. Name-calling and comparisons to hogs was pure meanness.

"They hurt your feelings." She didn't know why she felt the need to defend him.

He managed a smile that did not reach his eyes. "My skin's pretty thick. Growing up in foster care will do that."

Okay, now she really felt bad for him. The victory she wanted to celebrate fell flat. Hurting someone for gain wasn't her idea of a good win.

Wrestling with a myriad of disquieted emotions, she recentered on the most important reasons she had to sell this house, whether John-Parker's feelings were hurt or not. Her kids.

"Don't go behind my back again." She tried to sound forceful but failed. Sympathy would do that. "We're supposed to work together."

"Right. Work together. Cooperate. So, how about that coffee? I brought fresh-out-of-the-oven cinnamon rolls." He tapped his chest. "My part."

"Does that mean my part is coffee?"

This time his smile showed in his eyes. "Yours is better than mine. Much better."

Another compliment. Was he trying to win her over with compliments or was he a genuinely thoughtful man?

Who wanted to take away her hope.

"Does this mean you're giving up the idea of a halfway house?"

His eyes rolled toward the ceiling in exasperation.

"Foster home. A *home,* Zoey, for rejected boys. No, I'm not giving up. If I have to hire a lawyer, I will. Miss Mamie would want her legacy to continue." He placed the plastic tubs on the floor. "Where are my little buddies?"

A lawyer? She didn't have the money for a court battle.

So the victory she hadn't even celebrated wasn't a victory at all. Yet.

"Olivia's asleep and Owen's playing in the den with his Lego set. Why?"

About that time, Owen came racing into the living room,

dark hair sticking up in back, and slammed into John-Parker's legs. "Did you bring presents?"

"Owen," Zoey gasped and, in a tone intended to make her intentions clear, said, "Do not ever ask anyone but me for presents. Never."

Stricken, her son, looked up at the tall man. "But he likes me, don't you, Mr. John-Parker?"

John-Parker pumped his eyebrows. "That's a fact, my man. How about a doughnut?" Then, as if he remembered who was in charge, he looked at her. "If Mom says it's okay."

"Mom, can I have a doughnut? I be nice all day."

John-Parker chuckled and patted her son's back. "You're always nice. That's what I like about you."

"Mom's nice, too, isn't she?"

Zoey snickered. "Pushed you into a corner, didn't he?"

"You are nice. When you want to be." She was pretty sure his eyes twinkled. "Like when you make your delicious coffee to go with these hot doughnuts."

Stifling a laugh, Zoey extended both palms. "All right, all right, but I'm still mad about your underhanded play last night."

"Me, too."

"Yeah, you're sorry it failed."

He laughed, and she couldn't help herself. She let go of the laugh she'd stifled seconds before.

John-Parker had that effect on her. One minute she wanted to clobber him and the next he made her laugh.

Maybe he wasn't such a bad guy. Perhaps his reasons for disappearing for fifteen years were legitimate. Maybe he truly regretted the absence from Mamie's life.

And there she went making excuses for him.

With a huff of irritation at herself, Zoey headed for the kitchen to start the coffee he kept nagging about.

John-Parker followed. Owen, seated on the man's shiny boot, wrapped both arms around John-Parker's leg.

Walking with a thirty-pound, three-year-old clinging like a koala didn't take much effort for John-Parker.

But watching them pressed an old bruise in Zoey's chest.

Regret. Yearning to go back in time and make wiser choices.

Her son lacked an engaged man in his life. Even his late father had been too busy—mostly with other women—to pay his son much attention. She doubted Owen remembered Vic at all.

She wished she didn't.

When the coffee was brewed and smelling up the kitchen like a Starbucks, the three of them settled at the table to hash out more plans for the house.

Other than the basic kitchen area, the main floor of the house was packed and most already donated or discarded. The furniture other than her and the kids' necessities was gone. The unused portion of the upstairs had been cleared out and only the basement remained untouched.

They'd accomplished a lot in a few weeks.

John-Parker had contacted contractors for bids on the areas they couldn't address themselves. She had used her bookkeeping skills to set up a tentative budget, and they'd agreed to tackle the major renos like the kitchen and bathrooms first.

John-Parker took a man-size bite of cinnamon roll, chewed and swallowed. "Man, that's good." He sipped his coffee. "I have an idea to run past you."

"No."

He laughed. "You can't discourage me any more than I already am, so hear me out. The basement is a perfect place for a rec room."

"A family home doesn't need a rec room."

"Sure it does. Huge selling point. I talked to Pam, the local Realtor, and she agrees. A finished basement adds value. The plumbing is there from the washer and dryer to add a bathroom and a kitchenette. Buyers can decide if they want the space to be a mother-in-law suite, an ADU-accessory dwelling unit," he explained before continuing, " a rec room, bedrooms—anything they want."

"I'm warming to the idea, although I see your devious plot. A basement would also be a great place for rowdy teenagers to work off energy if you manage to change the council's minds."

John-Parker pointed at her. "You're brilliant. What a great idea. Thank you for thinking of it."

Eyes narrowed, she scowled, half joking, half serious. "You're incorrigible."

"Not anymore, but I used to be." He said the words easily, almost flippantly, but his expression was sincere, even penitent. "Miss Mamie and Jesus saved me."

Levity fled. His occasional mentions of Jesus bothered her. If she was honest, they made her mad. "I'm not much on Jesus, but Mamie was great."

"What do you have against Jesus?"

"I tried to believe in God for Mamie's sake, but when I look at my life and her illness, where was He?"

"Did Mamie ever stop believing in Him? Even when she was sick?"

"No, but that's my point. She believed, and tons of people prayed for her, but she still died."

"We all die, Zoey. This world is not our final destination. Knowing Jesus gives me assurance that mine will be with Him in the most perfect place imaginable."

"That's still not a good answer."

"I know." He reached across the table and placed a strong hand over hers. "I know, but I also know the peace and security I never had until I let Him into my life."

"So now your life is all perfect and full of roses?" She knew she sounded bitter. She was.

"Not even close. But Jesus is. As long as I focus on Him instead of my circumstances, I can trust that everything will work out the way He wants it to."

"Nice for you, but not for me." She pulled her hand from beneath his. The last thing she wanted was a sermon. From him, of all people. "We should get to work."

Taking her coffee cup and Owen's milk glass, she carried them to the sink. Her insides wadded in a tangle, she stared out the window toward the quiet, older neighborhood, wishing Mamie was still here. Wishing this man who bothered her too much had stayed in Phoenix. Wishing her life, her past, was different.

She doubted anyone had the kind of peace he talked about, but if such confidence existed, she envied it.

A car pulled to the curb. Thankfully. A distraction from John-Parker and the turmoil boiling inside her. "I have company."

"Ah, yes. They're here." John-Parker scraped back from the table and started toward the living room. Owen hopped down and tagged along.

"Did you know someone with two teenage boys was coming here?" she asked, following him.

"I invited them. Children's Services is loaning us some teenagers from a transitional home in Centerville who could use a part-time job."

"Children's Services? I'm not sure I want them around my children." Was the man out of his head? A couple of troubled teens in her house, mouthing off, showing her kids a bad example? Owen had had enough male negativity when he was Olivia's age.

"Just meet them, Zoey. Give them a chance. One day. That's all I promised to the social worker. If they give you grief, they're out of here."

"You'd better watch them like a hawk." She poked a finger at him. "Every minute."

He caught her finger, his gaze sincere. "Done. Promise. Trust me."

Her mouth twisted with scorn. "Right. Trust the man who wants to steal my inheritance."

"A man with a different plan. No stealing." Something in his tight smile said she'd hit a sore spot.

John-Parker opened the door and met the newcomers in a

front yard that needed mowing. Maybe he'd put the boys to work out there, away from her and the children.

Owen squeezed around her and went to John-Parker, who pulled her son up tight against his jeans-clad leg as he spoke to the social worker and shook hands with the boys.

With a huff of annoyance, Zoey walked out into the yard. One swear word, one smart remark, and those two were out of here.

Zoey wasn't happy with him or his big ideas.

As soon as he and the teens had formulated a plan to clear out the basement, she'd insisted that a protesting Owen attend a Mother's Day Out program at Mamie's church. For a woman who claimed not to trust in Jesus, she was quick to use His people.

His conscience pinged. Zoey was a wounded soul, the same as he'd been. He should pray for her instead of criticizing.

God was funny like that. From His upside-down viewpoint, God expected believers to love and pray for their enemies. John-Parker could think of several people he'd have to pray for whether he wanted to or not. Love them? Well, he was still working on that part.

By the time Zoey returned from the church, sans both kids, John-Parker had spent enough time with the teenagers to peg each one.

River, a fifteen-year-old with stringy black hair to his shoulders, carried a chip as big as a boulder. He reminded John-Parker of Rio, and the similar names were not lost on him. *Rio* meant river in Spanish, a language John-Parker had learned from living in Arizona and working in Central and South America. Like his namesake, River required special handling. Street smart and suspicious, he'd see through a con or take advantage of a weakness in seconds.

The younger boy, Charlie, had a gentle spirit, a need to

please, but lacked confidence. He stuck close to River, looking to him before making a decision.

John-Parker had once been that connected with Rio, following the lead of the slightly older, more streetwise boy.

That hadn't turned out so well. But it had given him the knowledge of how to redirect a sweet kid like Charlie.

These boys needed a mentor, a role model, especially slightly chubby, baby-faced Charlie. John-Parker was willing to be that man, if the boys would let him.

John-Parker stopped himself in mid thought. He wouldn't be here long enough to make a major difference. He couldn't take on a mentoring róle, nor could he remain in Rosemary Ridge and run a foster home. With the town council against him, he couldn't even get the place off the ground for someone else to run.

What had he been thinking?

But he knew. The pressure in his chest that meant God was leading him down an unknown road. The same pressure that had led him and Brandt to start the security agency.

Whether he knew how things would work out or not, he had to keep moving in that direction. God was in charge of the ultimate destination.

The only way to redemption was forward.

But how? How did he please Mamie and the Lord while living his own life in Phoenix? He couldn't give up his hard-earned business in Phoenix. God wouldn't expect that, would He? A man had to make a living. Silent Security was his life's work and all he knew.

What exactly *did* God expect of him?

While turning the thoughts over and over in his mind, John-Parker handed the stringy-haired River a box of junk. "Take that out to the big trash bin."

He'd rented an industrial trash receptacle for the duration of the project. Kitchen and bath demo would fill most of it, jobs the boys would probably enjoy if today went well.

"What are we doing this for anyway?" River, thin, bony shoulders defensive, took the box none too willingly.

Charlie elbowed him. "Money, River. The dude's paying us."

"If you've changed your mind about working for me, I'll give the social worker a call. Your choice." Hands loose at his sides, John-Parker met River's eyes and held on until the boy looked away.

Boys like River—like he'd been, too—needed a strong hand. Strong and consistent, as well as caring. John-Parker knew a thing or two about learning discipline. If he was a pushover, he'd lose the kid before they even started. Mamie had showed him that. The woman had never been anyone's pushover.

Charlie picked up another box marked for trash. "Come on, River, this is better than being stuck in a facility cleaning toilets."

"I guess." With a slouch that showed his opinion of himself more than of the world, the youth started up the steps. "Creepy down here anyway."

John-Parker chuckled, calling behind him, "It won't be when we finish. This will be an awesome rec room for the boys who live here."

River paused halfway up to look back over his shoulder. Hair flopped over his dark eyes. "Yeah? You got boys?"

"I will have. Maybe even you."

River's face shuttered. "Yeah, right."

Watching him go, John-Parker knew he had work to do to bring River around. Hard work. Charlie, at fourteen, was softer, easier. River, like Rio, had been moved around in the system too long.

*Guide me, Jesus.*

Hadn't he prayed that prayer many times since coming to a saving grace through Jesus? The Lord had never failed him. *He'd* failed, but God never had.

"I don't want to fail these boys, Lord," he murmured.

"Huh?" Charlie, halfway to the stairs, stopped and turned around. "Did you say something?"

Did he dare tell the boy he was praying? Would the admission send Charlie into a shell or interest him?

"I was praying."

The boy stared at him for a few beats of time. Then he swallowed. Hard. "My granny used to pray. Before she died."

"Did you live with your granny?"

Charlie nodded, the sadness in his eyes penetrating John-Parker's heart.

"When did she pass?"

"About two years ago. That's why I'm in foster care." Charlie shrugged as if he didn't care when it was apparent he hurt like crazy. "Nobody wants a twelve-year-old nuisance. They sure don't want a fourteen-year-old. There's lots of us, you know."

John-Parker knew. Oh, yes, he knew. He also knew the bewildered pain of rejection. "You're not a nuisance, Charlie. People just don't know you yet."

When the boy didn't respond, he went on. "Thanks for helping me with this basement."

"Can I work for you again? I'm saving for basketball shoes."

"You play ball?"

"I want to be ready when school starts again."

In other words, Charlie hadn't played basketball this year because he didn't have appropriate shoes.

Stuff like that shouldn't happen to a kid. Charlie would have those shoes whether he worked for John-Parker or not.

"We'll see how today goes, Charlie. But there's plenty to do around here, including demo, yardwork, a garden to plant. Work hard, behave yourself, and you'll earn those shoes and more."

Without a word, as if he didn't quite believe John-Parker, the boy disappeared up the stairs, carrying a box of trash and a whole lot of internal garbage that only God could remove.

## *Chapter Eight*

On Sunday, John-Parker joined his Phoenix church online, leaving his lonely rental behind to hang out at Mamie's place. Every minute he could be with Zoey was a minute to convince her that his plan was the right one. He needed her, especially with the council against him.

Manipulative, perhaps, but necessary.

Never mind that the stubborn, fiery woman was starting to grow on him. He even enjoyed matching wits with her.

And he really liked her kids. He, who knew next to nothing about children, was growing attached to Owen and Olivia. Especially Owen.

Bizarrely true, as Brandt often said when truth was stranger than fiction.

He and his partner had spoken by video last night, sorting out office kinks. As best friends do, they'd fallen into a discussion of Mamie, her house and his big idea. Brandt thought he was a glutton for pain to be in Rosemary Ridge for three months, but as was his quiet way, he supported the idea of helping other teens such as the two of them had been. Alone. Abandoned.

Brandt's rejection went far deeper than his. John-Parker's family was dead. Brandt's was not.

They'd ended the call with prayer, two strong men who knew that the source of their strength did not come from frequent gym workouts.

Now, this morning, as Zoey roamed in and out of the soon-to-be-demolished kitchen, John-Parker settled at the table.

Owen climbed on his lap, fascinated by the mobile tablet.

Zoey, Olivia on her hip, paused at the sink for a glass of water. "Leave John-Parker alone, Owen."

John-Parker looked up at her. She looked tired. Pretty but tired.

When had he started thinking she was pretty?

"The boy's okay. I like his company. We're buds, right, pal?"

Owen beamed up at his mother. "We're buds, Mom."

Her mouth quivered. The boy was a charmer.

"Okay." To John-Parker she said, "If he's too much trouble, send him upstairs to me."

"Sure, but that won't happen." He tapped the live stream from his church's website and contemporary music flowed from the device.

Zoey came over to the table and peeked over his shoulder. "I thought you were ordering supplies for the house."

Olivia reached a chubby hand toward him. John-Parker gave her fingers a gentle shake.

"Did that last night. Today is Sunday. Church."

"Oh." This time her face didn't close up as if she'd eaten a sour pickle. "You're not going to Aunt Mamie's church at South Cross?"

"Maybe next week. When I have some company?" He lifted both eyebrows, hopeful but not surprised when her answer came.

"You know my feelings on that."

"What about Owen? Will you let me take him?"

She hesitated for a few seconds. "I'll think about it."

Then, after one long look at her son, she took her water glass and her baby and left the room.

John-Parker hoped, prayed, she'd return and join them.

Ten minutes into the lively praise worship, she came back downstairs. He said nothing and didn't look her way but he was aware of her presence. She fiddled around in the kitchen, occasionally passing by the table and the computer.

Owen patted his hands to the music and followed John-Parker's lead when he bowed his head in prayer…and dug his sweetness deeper into John-Parker's heart.

Did his mother notice? He hoped so.

To be raising such a good little boy, Zoey must be a good mom, even if she seemed determined to treat John-Parker like a leper.

Sometimes.

Sometimes she appeared to like him. She even laughed at his lame comments. Once she'd bumped his shoulder with hers on purpose and teased him about the demo dust on his shiny boots. She'd already pegged him as picky about keeping his footwear clean.

Puzzling woman.

He understood some of the reasons for her animosity. Who wouldn't distrust his intentions after his fifteen-year failure? She blamed him for abandoning Mamie, although no more than he blamed himself. Now, she resented his intrusion.

He'd messed up. Failed. Hurt the one person who'd never failed him. Then he'd roared back into town to play the conquering hero and cluttered Zoey's plans for the future.

No wonder she didn't trust him.

She passed by the table again, trailing the scent of kitchen spices. Was she cooking? Curious about the church service? Checking on her son to be sure the bad man from Arizona didn't corrupt him?

Knowing she thought the worst of him, bothered him. He'd been the object of false opinions for half his life. Apparently, he still was, courtesy of the town council and Zoey. But how did he prove he was no longer that mixed-up kid? And why did he care what she thought? He had other things to think about, including the teenage boys and the good he wanted to do in this house.

He toyed with the thought of building a basketball court in the backyard to go along with finishing out the basement. Great ideas. Boys needed outlets for their anger and energy to keep them out of trouble.

Other ideas, some from Brandt last night, crowded into his head.

He'd need to appeal to Zoey's good side to make any of those happen. And the budget, of course, although Lonnie Buckner had yet to reveal exactly how extensive that was.

As executor to Mamie's will, the attorney wanted to see the completed reno plans first.

John-Parker was working on them. If Zoey would cooperate.

The weeks had flown past. He and Zoey had to settle things soon. Like now. Today. The architect had ideas, but those ideas required decisions from two conflicting voices. His and Zoey's.

*Guide me, Lord.*

The simple prayer brought him back to the online church, where his focus should be.

When the service ended, John-Parker tapped the tablet closed. At some point in his musings, Zoey had left the kitchen again. With Owen at his side, they went in search of her.

They found her sitting on the floor beside an upstairs closet with Olivia nearby and a pile of file folders scattered around her. She glanced up when he and Owen came inside.

"Look what I found." She held up a lavender-colored journal. "One of Aunt Mamie's old journals."

"I didn't know she kept a journal." He wanted to grab the book from her hand as if holding Mamie's words of wisdom could somehow exonerate his guilt. He didn't, of course. A book wouldn't erase fifteen years of neglect.

"Me either." Zoey pressed the journal to her chest, eyes glassy. "May I keep it?"

As much as he wanted to read Mamie's words for himself, John-Parker couldn't refuse. Not with Zoey staring at him from dark brown eyes filled with grief and need.

Had she cared more for her aunt than he'd originally thought?

"Keep anything you want, Zoey," he said gently. "If you find something interesting—anything that reveals why she included me in the will—tell me. Okay?"

Because he was right back to square one. Fifteen years apart, so why him?

Zoey held the journal against her chest, her heart full to have this gift from Mamie.

"So you wonder, too?"

John-Parker dipped his chin. "I told you that at the lawyer's office." He spoke without rancor, his tone calm and agreeable.

Zoey dropped her gaze to the pile of rubble and papers on the floor, suddenly ashamed of that day's behavior. "I was shocked and upset. I don't remember much."

"Shocking for both of us." He went to his haunches and drove a Hot Wheels' Jeep over Owen's foot and up to his knee. The boy giggled; a sweet, happy sound that did a mother's heart good.

Owen loved when John-Parker paid attention to him. His calm, patient manner put her usually shy son at ease.

Except for that rough day in the lawyer's office, the man had an uncanny peacefulness about him, as if nothing, not even her accusations, could cause him to strike out at her.

Was that what he'd meant by the peace he felt from Jesus?

Was that what he got from watching an online church service? She had to admit she'd liked the music. And watching Owen clap his hands and bow his head with John-Parker had almost made her cry.

"I was rude to you that day," she said.

"Maybe I was rude, too."

"Maybe? You accused me of being one of those women who move in on older people and steal their money."

His mouth opened, as if he wanted to say more on the topic, but after a pause, he said, "If I was wrong, I apologize."

"You were."

An ornery twinkle accompanied the quiver of a grin. "I repeat. I apologize. If you do."

Grudgingly, with a flutter of one hand, as if to brush away the conflict that seemed to flare at every opportunity, Zoey answered, "Okay. I apologize, too. Peace, truce, and all that jazz."

Leaning sideways toward her daughter, she rescued a piece of paper from Olivia's hands. "She'll eat anything she finds."

John-Parker folded his long legs beneath him and joined her on the floor. "Want some help?"

"I'm cleaning out the file cabinet Mamie kept locked in this closet."

"Important documents?"

"Some. I found her foster licenses and home studies going back for years. Here's the title to her minivan." She handed the document to him. "What should we do with her car?"

"Keep it?"

"I have a car. You have a truck."

"We might need a van." The man tried, but failed, to look innocent. Obviously, he had an agenda, and Zoey suspected what it was.

"If you're thinking you need a van to haul teenagers in, I object."

He held up both hands, long fingers spread wide. "In the interest of our recent truce treaty, I table the motion. For now. But I do have some ideas to run past you while we work."

"As long as they're ideas to generate a bigger sale price, I'm all ears."

"The backyard is large. We have room for your garden, a workshop, a finished basketball court, and more."

"I've changed my mind about the garden. Gardens don't add value. A workshop, maybe." Men buyers especially would be drawn to a place to do whatever men did in a workshop. Storage for the lawnmower, tools, bicycles, too. She could see the benefit. "A basketball court? I don't see the point of investing money there."

"Teenagers like them. So do adults. Regardless of which of us gets our way about the house's future, people will live here. Moms and dads with their kids, whether foster or traditional, want a backyard to do things in."

Stubborn man. Still, his argument was sensible. She made a face at him for good measure.

Agreeing on something was progress, even if they had differing opinions for the ultimate end.

With the clock ticking, they'd have to compromise. A lot.

But she certainly didn't plan do all the compromising by herself.

"Show me photos or drawings of what you have in mind," she said. "Can we afford to build or purchase an outbuilding, and will the town council approve it?"

"They don't have to. I checked. An outbuilding does not require a permit." He slapped his hands together. "Bam! Finally, a win for my team."

Both little ones looked up, startled by the sudden clap, eyes wide. Zoey's heart pinched at that reaction that had yet to go away. Olivia hadn't lived in turmoil, but Owen had, and he still jumped at loud noises.

No matter what she had to do, her babies would never experience that again.

"Zoey, we can do this." John-Patrick reached for her hand. She shocked herself by letting him take hold. "Think of the lives this house can change for the better, just as it made a difference for you and me."

She wished he'd stop saying that. He was right. She knew he was. And his constant reminders ate at her conscience, just as his touch ate away at her determination to never, ever, let another man into her life.

John-Parker was wearing her down. In more ways than one.

Pulse bumping, she slid her fingers from his and closed her hand into a fist.

If they didn't sell the house, where would she get the money to buy or rent a little home for her children? Her online job didn't generate enough income for so much as a down payment. And paying for daycare would eat into any added money a full-time job would bring in. Anyway, she wanted to raise her children herself, not relegate them to someone else's care most of their waking hours. Like so many other mothers, she might not have a choice, but she had to try.

"Do you still want a rec room?" To quiet the worry giving her a headache, Zoey focused on the here and now. She could do nothing about the future. Yet. "I'm not sold on spending so much money on a basement."

"I may have a better idea."

"Oh, boy." She pretended to roll her eyes. "More of your ideas."

"Seriously, Zoey, you need that basement."

"*I* do?"

"Where will you live when construction starts?"

"I thought the kids and I could remain upstairs until the downstairs was finished and then switch."

"There's no kitchen upstairs."

"We'll manage."

"How?"

There he went, being reasonable. Practical. And thoughtful. As if he cared that she and the kids had what they needed. The thoughtfulness disconcerted her. "I don't know, but we will. We have to."

He touched her knee. "No, you don't. Zoey, the basement is the perfect place for you."

She pretended shock, knowing he did not mean that the way it sounded. "You're going to lock us in the basement? I knew we were enemies, but that's downright diabolical."

He laughed, as she'd intended, before growing serious again. "We're not enemies, Zoey."

No, they weren't. And she wasn't sure what to do with that.

"You need a place to live during the renovation. You've already admitted you're short of funds and rentals aren't cheap. I propose we focus on turning the basement into an apartment immediately. Then you and the kids can live down there while the rest of the house is finished."

The offer surprised her and, to be honest, gave her a little thrill. Not only because it solved a problem for her, but because John-Parker had thought of it. "Why would you do that for me?"

"Because I'm not the bad guy you'd like me to be. Besides—" he grinned as if he couldn't let the conversation be too serious "—more bedrooms mean we can help more kids."

She shook her head, amused at his dogged focus but touched that he'd been thinking of her and her kids, not just the teenagers in foster care.

Every hour she spent with John-Parker Wisdom was an hour more of noticing his kindness to her kids, to the teenage boys, to her. Of laughing at his wit. Of wanting him to notice her as more than co-heir to Mamie's estate.

Some days she thought he did. Like now, when he held her hand and gazed at her with gray-eyed sincerity.

The only things that kept her from doing something ridiculous like falling for him, were the house and the fifteen lonely years Mamie had spent worrying about him.

Attraction aside, her kids came first.

Swallowing hard against the sudden flood of emotions and refocused on her mission, Zoey slid her hand from his.

"More beds and baths mean a bigger sale price, too." She widened her eyes at him in a gotcha expression. "Did you think of that?"

John-Parker sat back, grinning. "So you're on board with being locked in the basement? Awesome."

She snorted. "I didn't say that."

"Oh, I think you did. Didn't she, Owen?" His gray eyes danced.

"Leave my innocent child out of this!" The man was as charmingly funny as he was troublesome.

The boy's gaze ping-ponged between the two adults. "Are you mad? I don't want locked up."

"No, buddy. No." Before she had a chance to reassure her son, John-Parker pulled him onto his knee. "Your mom and I are joking around, having fun. No one's getting locked anywhere. Right, Mom?"

"Right. We're talking about the house, and John-Parker was teasing Mom. We're not mad a bit."

She put her hands over Owen's ears and whispered to John-Parker. "He's heard too much arguing in his life."

Something deep and knowing shifted over him, all teasing aside. In a quiet voice filled with emotion, mouth tight, he murmured, "Never again, not from me, not in his presence."

Zoey's heart squeezed with sensations she'd not expected to feel for this man. Gratitude. Affection. Comradery.

First the basement living quarters and now his concern for her child.

John-Parker Wisdom was right. He was a much nicer man than she'd given him credit for.

Another week went by. The warmth of June edged toward the scalding heat of July. Two months left to do the near impossible, especially with so many critical players against him.

Demo progressed, contractors arrived with bids, and John-Parker hashed out deals with as many as he thought they could afford. The rest he, Zoey and the teenagers would tackle.

Zoey had agreed to building a workshop if it was in budget, and he still argued for the garden, surprised that she was against it. She loved working in her flowers and vegetables and sharing the early harvest with neighbors and friends. She also sold the peas, asparagus and carrots to the local farmers market for extra money. Money she and those kids needed.

She loved that garden, generously shared it, and he liked hearing her sing as she pulled weeds and harvested the bounty.

Yesterday, he'd wasted fifteen minutes secretly watching through a window as she'd patiently showed Owen how to plant another row of radish seeds.

She was going to keep her garden. At least for this year.

Next year remained murky.

Leaving his increasingly lonely rental with his usual phone schedule and list of errands, he headed into town for breakfast with the folks at the Drugstore Café.

Taste buds alive with hunger, he entered to the powerful scents of bacon and coffee.

As usual, the business was crowded. Several people nodded or spoke as he passed. He paused here and there to say hello, hat in hand, putting a friendly face with his plans.

The more he presented himself as a solid citizen to the townspeople, the less trouble he'd have over fostering a houseful of teenage boys. He had to convince the council to waive the nuisance ordinance and if he had to glad-hand everyone in town, he would.

Manipulative, no. Strategic, yes.

If Rosemary Ridge remembered his misspent youth, most said nothing. He suspected they watched him a little closer, wondered about him, but he hadn't heard the derisive street rat moniker since the council meeting.

The newspaper editor, Clare, along with Zoey's interesting photographer friend, Taffy, smiled at him from across the crowded room. The woman frequented Mamie's house and whisked Zoey away occasionally on trips to who knew where. Zoey always came back happy, so John-Parker had decided to like Taffy even if she had threatened to kneecap him if he caused any grief to her bestie.

He'd laughed. Taffy had not.

He was still amused. But cautious. Newspaper people wielded power that he needed in his favor.

John-Parker also spotted a few other familiar faces, contractors, business people, including the florist. She stopped him as he passed. "I'll have that flower arrangement ready this afternoon."

"Thanks." The reminder put a lump in his throat. Tomorrow was the fourth-month anniversary of Mamie's death.

"John-Parker." He heard his name called and followed the sound to the pair he was looking for. Frank and Wink, the two old guys who must have been around during his teen years. But what self-centered teenager ever noticed older people?

He sure hadn't. Now, he appreciated the entertaining pair and their easy friendship.

"You've become quite the regular, my boy." Frank Myrick, in his usual denim overalls, pushed a chair away from the table with his foot. "Saved you a spot."

The server, Penny, waved two fingers and lifted the coffee carafe along with her eyebrows. John-Parker nodded and flipped over the white mug already in place on the table.

"She's got her eye on you, John-Parker," Wink muttered.

"Ah, Wink," Frank put in, "he's a big tipper. That's what Penny's after."

As always, the two old guys made him smile. "Guess I've lost my charm."

Frank scoffed. "The way I see it, that charm of yours is highly focused on a certain pretty, dark-haired mama at Mamie's place."

"Zoey?" He blinked. "We're just working together."

Wink snickered. "Not the way I see it. You jabber on about that woman worse than a teenage boy with a big crush."

"No, I don't." *Do I?*

"We know more about her now than we ever did before." Wink wiggled his speckled eyebrows. "She's a great mama, reads to her babies, teaches them about the garden, loves on them."

Had he told them all that?

"Yep," Frank added. "She's smart, too, great with numbers, which you claim not to be. Made a budget for the remodel. Works hard all day every day."

He'd been thinking out loud, organizing his thoughts. That was all. "Maybe I talk too much."

"Only about her. And them kiddos."

Penny arrived with Wink's and Frank's breakfast. She turned a dazzling smile on John-Parker. "Yours is almost ready, John-Parker. Would you like extra biscuits for the gravy?"

Beside him, Wink hummed beneath his breath.

"That would be great. Thanks. Put them on my bill."

She winked. "On the house."

When she left, Wink shook out his napkin with a flourish. "Told you."

"I won't be in town that long," John-Parker said, relieved to know it was true. Even though Penny was pretty and friendly, he couldn't get involved.

Zoey's face flashed through his head.

With her either. Even if he thought about her often and maybe talked about her more than he should.

She didn't return the favor. Or did she?

In a month's time, he and Zoey had come a long way. At least, she no longer behaved as if he was something on the bottom of her shoe.

"Back to our conversation," Frank said, pointing a forkful of ham at John-Parker.

John-Parker groaned. "Not Zoey."

"Why not? You like to talk about her. According to you, she's a regular Florine Nightshade, visiting old folks at the nursing home, especially the ones without families. Makes them cards and treats, takes the little ones to cheer up the old folks."

"Florence Nightingale," Wink corrected as John-Parker smiled into his coffee.

"I still wonder about the nursing home trips," he said.

"Wonder? What's there to wonder? The woman is a tender heart."

"You're right. She is." Probably.

John-Parker hadn't intended to voice his doubts, but the thought alternately rolled through his head along with thoughts of how much he liked being with her. Did Zoey truly have a soft spot for the elderly? John-Parker prayed she did and wasn't on the search for another elderly mark as a backup plan in case they didn't sell the house.

The Myrick brothers were correct.

He'd developed a soft spot for Zoey Chavez.

# Chapter Nine

For several days after that, John-Parker fretted over the conversation with Wink and Frank, and he also guarded his speech more closely.

As he'd told them, he wouldn't be here long enough to start a relationship, especially with a woman he barely trusted. A woman on his mind pretty much all the time, although he was convinced this was because of the will and the house, not because he found her attractive. Even if he did.

To deny he liked Zoey a lot would be a lie and he did not lie, even to himself. When two people spend every day together, they either become friends or enemies.

He didn't believe in making enemies.

Being with Zoey was too exhilarating and fun, even when they argued.

How was that for a conundrum?

One afternoon while he explored the recently discovered treasure trove of old furniture, dusty suitcases and plastic bins in the attic, Zoey called up to him.

"Your boys are here."

His boys.

The term felt right. The Lord had called him to mentor these boys while he was in Rosemary Ridge, especially River, the most troubled. If he could plant the seeds of faith, character and responsibility, God would send someone else to water them and help them grow.

He climbed down from the attic and made his way to the porch. Only River exited the social worker's vehicle, citing homework for Charlie. The boys were behind in school and even though they complained about the extra work, they had no choice except to attend summer school.

River either had completed his work or lied about it. Rio

would have. Then, even without turning in one assignment, he'd ace the tests. Mamie had said he was too smart for his own good. River reminded John-Parker of Rio so much, he'd almost called him by that name a couple of times.

He prayed for them both every day.

When the social worker drove away, John-Parker motioned toward his truck.

"Load up."

Suspicion flared, River's first reaction to any command. "Where we going?"

"Errands. Hardware store."

The boy gave a don't-care shrug but climbed into the vehicle.

As they drove to town, the cab was quiet. River stared straight ahead, the chip on his shoulder weighing him down.

"How's everything, River?"

"Okay."

"School?"

"Boring. Dumb."

"What did you learn today?"

"Nothing." The shaggy-haired boy turned in the seat to glare at John-Parker. "What is this? An interrogation?"

"Big word."

"I ain't as dumb as you think."

"No, you aren't." He accented the word *aren't*. River knew the correct grammar. He chose not to use it. "I figured that out. What do you like to do for fun?"

"Nothing."

"Charlie says you're an artist."

"He talks too much."

"But you like him and look out for him. I appreciate that."

"He's all right. Whines about his dead granny too much, but he's just a kid. Needy."

*Like you*, John-Parker thought. A needy kid, half grown and hurting. Mad at the world for cheating him out of a stable childhood.

"What about you? Do you miss your granny or someone else in your family?"

"My mom, I guess."

This was his first mention of family, which gave John-Parker hope that the boy wouldn't be stuck in foster care until he turned eighteen. "Do you get to see her?"

"What do you think? I been in the system most of my life. I live with my mom a while then come back here. Over and over. I can take care of myself, but no one believes me. It stinks."

"Yes, it does."

"Mom says she's getting clean for good this time."

"Do you believe her?"

"No." River shifted in the seat and made a disgruntled sound. "I don't know. Maybe. She's got clean before, but her creepy boyfriend drags her back down. It's his fault. If she'd get rid of him, I could live with her and help her stay clean. We'd be okay."

John-Parker heard the pain and rage beneath River's words. He couldn't blame his mother, so he blamed the boyfriend, but deep down he knew the truth.

"You don't have to make the same choices."

River narrowed his eyes. "What do you think I am, a stupid little kid?"

Not stupid, but broken and confused.

Heart heavy, John-Parker pulled into the parking space outside the Green Brothers' Hardware and Lumber store. They were making a good living off him these days.

River reached for the door handle.

"Hold up, River." John-Parker killed the engine and turned toward the teen.

"I'm going to say something. You might not want to hear it, but it's the truth."

River didn't release the door handle, as if he'd bolt if John-Parker's words upset him.

"You gonna tell me to forget her? She's never gonna get clean and be a real mom? She's a hopeless loser? Like me."

"The very opposite. There's someone who can help your mom get clean and stay that way. Forever."

"Who? Some bigshot head doc? She's done that. Didn't work. He just gave her more drugs to take."

"There's a God in Heaven who loves your mom. We should make a pact to pray for her every day."

River rolled his eyes. "Oh, man, a preacher. You think talking to the sky fixes anything?"

"Talking to Jesus does. He fixed me."

"You? In your fancy truck and slick boots?"

"I didn't always have these things." He held the boy's gaze, hoping his sincerity came through. "I grew up in foster care in that house we're remodeling."

"You never told us that."

"I'm telling you now. The woman who cared for us in that house showed us through example that we could change, and that faith in God could heal. Jesus changed my heart, my mind, and my life."

River stared at him, unconvinced.

John-Parker held out a pleading hand. "What would it hurt to pray for your mom?" *Yourself, too.* "Prayer costs you nothing." *And gives you everything you need, if you'll let it.*

River pondered for a few beats while John-Parker refused to look away. Then, with a sniff to show how little he cared, he said, "Can't hurt, I guess, but don't tell the other guys. They'll think I've gone off the deep end."

"Deal. You can tell them when you're ready."

"Like never."

A smile tugged at the corners of John-Parker's mouth. "We'll see."

Once inside the hardware store, John-Parker kept a close, but subtle, watch on River. He didn't know the kid well enough to be certain his fingers weren't sticky. John-Parker had known plenty of boys, himself included, who'd had less than honest moments.

After gathering a basketful of odds and ends for the house, they headed to the checkout where the scent of freshly popped corn warmed the air.

"Help yourself. It's free." The ponytailed cashier motioned to the red machine where buttery popcorn heaped high under a warming light.

She didn't have to tell River twice. Boys, John-Parker knew, were always hungry.

"Want one, John-Parker?"

"Sounds good. Thanks."

The kid shook out a small white bag. "Can I take some to Zoey and Owen? Is Olivia too little?"

That River thought of those back at the house pleased John-Parker. There was a lot of good in that boy. Getting it to rise above his trauma was the challenge.

John-Parker looked toward the cashier. "Is that okay?"

"Take all you want." The cashier chuckled, eyes widened. "You've spent enough money in here to earn more than a few bags of corn."

"True." John-Parker returned her grin. "Thank you."

River, having heard the reply, was already scooping popcorn into bags, so John-Parker focused on checking out.

Another customer was in the adjacent lane. John-Parker hoped the man didn't see him. He didn't want a confrontation.

Earl Beck, the man with the bad attitude on the town council, turned, spotted John-Parker, and frowned. "You still in town?"

John-Parker's stomach tightened. He dipped his chin, determined to remain courteous and get out fast. "Mr. Beck."

Beck's narrowed gaze landed on River. John-Parker knew what the man saw. Stringy long hair, baggy pants. "What's that you got with you? Another street rat? Better check his pockets."

Both cashiers looked toward River, who froze, one hand on the scoop inside the popcorn machine, the other holding a white paper bag. Hurt turned to fury on the boy's face. He glared at Beck then tossed the scoop and bag aside and stormed out of the store.

Heat boiled up in John-Parker, lava-hot. Beck was a bully. John-Parker did not like bullies.

Tapping down the anger, a long-formed habit of self-discipline instilled by the military and a desire to run a successful business, he gathered his cloak of calm about him. He was calm, but cold as ice and twice as vehement.

In a deadly quiet voice he used on bad guys in the field, he said, "Mr. Beck, your behavior is inappropriate and reprehensible. You don't have to like me. You don't have to approve of my plans for Mamie Bezek's home. But do not, I repeat, do not ever again speak that way to anyone, especially a kid, in my presence."

"Are you threatening me?"

Still so quiet that no one but the cashiers could hear, he went on. "Let's call it a warning. I don't want trouble. And I won't start trouble. But if you do, you'll find more than you can handle."

Earl Beck's neck reddened. "Kids like that are the real trouble and you know it. The same as you were. Here you are again, playing high and mighty, when you're the same as them. Nice clothes and a cowboy hat don't change what you are." Beck sneered. "You think people don't remember you. Well, I do. And I won't stand for your kind to repopulate my town with more trash."

Though his pulse rattled like rocks in a can and blood pounded in his temples, John-Parker sucked in a calming breath.

"Not the time or place, Beck." Continuing in an ultraquiet tone to the cashier, John-Parker said, "I apologize. This will never happen again. Total me up, please."

Looking shell-shocked and embarrassed, the cashier nodded.

Beck, his sale completed, took his plastic bag and stormed out of the store with one final glare at John-Parker.

When his supplies were sacked, John-Parker pushed the loaded basket toward the double-glass doors, eager to find River, praying the boy hadn't run off. Not that he could blame him.

"Sir," a feminine voice called behind him.

John-Parker turned to see the young cashier coming at him with her hands full of white bags. "The boy forgot his popcorn."

Some of his tension fled. Kindness went a long way; a lesson he'd learned in this town, though not from men like Beck.

"Thanks." He took the bags and settled them in the upper basket, though he'd lost his appetite completely. "I'm sorry about this."

"Not your fault."

He wished he believed that.

The drive home was quiet for a full three blocks. River didn't talk, didn't munch the popcorn, and kept his face turned toward the passenger window.

John-Parker had to try, although the damage was done. "River, none of that was about you." When River didn't answer, he went on. "Beck doesn't like me. He thinks I stole something from him a long time ago when I was a teenager."

River's head snapped around. "The statute of limitations is out by now, ain't it?"

John-Parker would have laughed if the situation had been different. Why had avoiding the law been River's first thought? Experience?

River's street smarts were showing again. Like Rio, his intellect needed positive direction.

"That's not the point. Beck shouldn't have included you in his dislike."

"I've heard his kind of trash talk before. People don't trust kids like me. Fine. No big deal."

Oh, but it was. The last thing River needed was more negativity. He believed the worst of himself already, just as Rio had. Even as John-Parker had at times, although Mamie had somehow imparted to him a smidgeon of self-esteem.

With a sigh and an inward prayer for guidance, John-Parker parked in the driveway. "Carry the popcorn to Zoey, okay?"

Without a reply, the boy took the bags and went inside. John-Parker followed with the supplies.

Hearing voices from the kitchen, he rounded the corner to find an elderly woman eating at the table. Zoey sat across from her, folding tea towels and making small talk.

John-Parker had never seen the stranger before. Maybe

one of Zoey's nursing home friends. The ugly thought that this woman could be her next mark shot through his brain. He erased it. The woman's clothes looked shabby and her hair could use a comb. He doubted she had a spare dollar.

"Hey, guys, did you—" Zoey stopped in midsentence. "What's wrong? You both look like a thunderstorm about to erupt."

John-Parker intentionally straightened his face. River wasn't quite as adept and continued to glower.

"Nothing to worry about. A little run-in with a naysayer."

"Oh." He could see the questions buzzing in her head but, with company present, Zoey didn't press.

"Here." River pushed the bags of popcorn toward her. "We brought popcorn."

"Oh, my, my," the old lady said, "I haven't had popcorn in a month of Sundays."

River shocked him sideways. "You can have mine."

"No, no." Withered, veined hands waved the air. "I didn't mean that, hon, but what a good boy you are." To John-Parker, she said, "Your son's a fine young man. You must be proud."

John-Parker saw the longing in River's face and dropped an arm around his shoulders. "I wish I could claim him, but I can't."

When the boy didn't move away or say anything negative, John-Parker went on. "It was River's idea to bring popcorn for everyone. Even Olivia."

"Who is too little to eat it." Zoey pushed a bag over to the older woman. "Calpernia, this bag is all yours."

"Well, then." Bony fingers gripped the white bag. "I wouldn't want it to go to waste. We don't get many treats on the street. Awful nice of you to bring me here."

"There's more casserole if you're still hungry, Calpernia. All you want."

"This corn tops me off good, hon. It's nice to sit in a real kitchen for a change and chat with another woman."

The conversation puzzled John-Parker. Who was this woman?

Zoey pushed to a stand. Above the stranger's head, she widened her eyes at John-Parker and slid them toward the woman. "John-Parker, if you and River will keep Calpernia company for a minute, Owen and I will check on her laundry in the dryer."

"Popcorn, Mom," Owen said and looked toward John-Parker.

Those brown eyes got him every time. "He can stay with me, too, if you don't care."

Zoey gnawed a corner of her mouth. "I don't want him to be a bother."

John-Parker picked up the boy and settled him on his lap at the table. "Couldn't happen."

"I'll be right back," she said, as though he and Owen hadn't hung out together dozens of times. Was it him she didn't trust? River? Or the old lady?

With a final glance, Zoey hurried toward the laundry room. John-Parker held the still-warm popcorn for Owen as he spoke to Calpernia. "I'm John-Parker Wisdom and this is River."

"I figured." Calpernia stuffed a handful of popcorn into her mouth.

Her movements stirred an unpleasant scent of body odor.

River, who was about to sit, too, backed away. "I got work in the basement. We're almost done down there."

John-Parker swallowed, looking for a similar escape. Except, he'd promised Zoey.

The old lady rocked a couple of times, though the kitchen chairs had no rockers. "She told me about you. Yes, sir."

She had? He'd like to have been in on that conversation.

"All bad, I guess," he joked.

Calpernia chortled. "Not hardly."

"John-Parker's nice. Mommy's nice, too. I love her."

"Calpernia reached out and patted the arm Owen had propped on the table. "She sure is. When we see her coming, everyone in the camp knows she's bringing food or blankets. Sometimes socks. Socks are hard to come by, you know."

Inside John-Parker's head, the tumblers began to fall in

place. Zoey was doing the woman's laundry, feeding her. Calpernia had mentioned the streets. Blankets, food, socks.

Was she homeless? Was that the community she spoke of? Did Zoey frequent the town's homeless camps?

Overwhelmed by Calpernia's odor, John-Parker lifted Owen to his feet and pushed away from the table.

"We need a glass of water. Popcorn's salty. Would you like some, ma'am?"

As good excuse as any.

Calpernia waved off the offer. "Zoey made tea. Sure was good, too. That woman of yours is a good soul. Yes, sir. A good soul."

Calpernia alternately repeated herself and shoved popcorn through a set of bad teeth.

John-Parker moved Owen to the opposite end of the long table and onto a booster chair.

"She's not my woman. We're…" What were they? Rivals? Acquaintances? Friends.

He settled at friendship, not willing to reach beyond. He'd misjudged her and that did not set well with a man who knew too much about being misjudged.

"She sure 'nuf talks about you with moony eyes. John-Parker this and John-Parker that. Why, I expected you to walk on water. Are you a Christian, boy? I sense it in my spirit."

"Yes, ma'am, I am."

"Mmm-hmm." Her body began to rock again. "I perceive you're here for a purpose. A purpose, yes, sir."

"I believe that." But how would this stranger know?

The rocking increased. Calpernia's eyes glazed as she seemed to stare at something beyond his shoulder.

"Be wise as serpents and gentle as doves, John-Parker Wisdom. The wolves will gather, but be strong in the Lord and His might. Not your own."

John-Parker recognized the jumbled bits of scripture, surprised that they'd come from this smelly old woman he'd never met before. What was she talking about? Where was this strange advice coming from?

"I will," he said, mostly to appease a woman he feared might be mentally ill or on drugs and unpredictable.

"Yes." She turned squinted eyes on him, eyes that blazed with a strange fire. "I believe you will. You are strong, yes, but a tender warrior. You will protect the lambs." She continued to rock. "Remember, though, what you think you've come to do may not be the same as your purpose. God has a plan."

John-Parker believed in God's plan with his whole heart, but he was convinced he already knew what that purpose was. To honor Mamie by giving teenage boys a home in this house.

How could this stranger know anything about him or his plans?

Unless Zoey had told her.

With a shudder, Calpernia rocked back in her chair and looked up at the stained ceiling. "The mystery. Yes, the mystery. It's all about the mystery."

Clearly, the old woman was confused. Probably had dementia.

Nevertheless, her words sent a chill down his back.

Later that evening, Zoey drove a freshly showered and well-fed Calpernia, along with clean clothes and a big pan of lasagna, to the homeless camp on the outskirts of town.

Although she'd invited the woman to spend the night, Calpernia had refused. She didn't like walls around her when she slept, but she wouldn't mind coming to visit again.

Heart sad for the woman and the others on the streets she befriended now and then, Zoey had promised to find her again if she could.

The homeless, she'd learned, moved around often. She seldom saw the same person twice.

If she was a praying woman, she'd pray that God would resolve the issues of the lonely, marginalized, homeless population. Living in squalor without adequate food and shelter for her children was Zoey's greatest fear. It could happen. Except for Mamie, it would have happened before.

An entry in Mamie's journal came to mind.

*Prayers once spoken last for eternity,* Mamie had written. *God stores them in golden bowls, forever to rise before Him like a sweet perfume.*

Zoey loved the beautiful sentiment even if she didn't believe prayers went anywhere, certainly not up to God to last forever. But she wanted to.

"God, if You're up there and care, keep Calpernia safe."

A waste of breath perhaps, but she felt better for saying the words out loud. There was comfort in thinking Calpernia's name would always be with God. Even it wasn't true.

Flummoxed by her unusual thoughts, Zoey drove home.

Back at the house, John-Parker continued to work through the attic, a complication she hadn't expected. They'd cleaned out the main floor and the basement, but the home she'd thought she knew so well was full of surprises. Including a bad roof. But framing on the basement was already underway, thanks to John-Parker, who had contractors lined up like dominoes. She had to admit, she appreciated his efficiency and attention to detail. The man was very organized.

On the drive home, Olivia had fallen asleep in the car. Zoey carried her up to the nursery, changed her and put her down for the night. Owen went in search of John-Parker.

"Tell him good-night and come back up. Okay?"

Owen wasn't one to argue, but this time he did. "I want John-Parker to play."

"You heard me. Go."

With a beleaguered sigh, her son went in search of his hero.

She worried about his attachment to the man. John-Parker would soon be gone. This first month had flown past quickly. Too quickly, if their progress on the house was any indication. John-Parker claimed things would hum along now that contractors were in place, but she worried anyway. They had to make the deadline and agree on what to do with the house. Or lose it completely.

She could not let that happen. Her children depended on her.

By the time she'd laid out Owen's pajamas, she heard him on the stairs, talking to John-Parker.

Owen's bedroom door was open so he and John-Parker came inside. Her son went directly to a low shelf, took down a favorite story, and handed the book to John-Parker.

"He asked me to read his bedtime story." Tall and oversize among the toddler furniture, John-Parker looked to her. "Is that okay with you?"

Zoey appreciated that he asked her permission instead of assuming he knew what was best for her kids. "Be my guest. Owen, go potty and get your pajamas on first."

Owen rushed to the bathroom and was back in a flash, his superhero pajama top on wrong side out. He wouldn't let her make the change. Only John-Parker.

The concern pressed in again. Owen needed a good man in his life. Not this one, though.

John-Parker was a better man than she'd expected, but he could not be her son's role model. Not for long.

Yet, as John-Parker's deep voice rumbled out the different characters in *Brown Bear, Brown Bear,* tenderness thickened beneath Zoey's ribs. For her son. And, yes, for John-Parker.

She wanted to lie down on the carpet, close her eyes and listen to that gentle rumble herself.

She didn't, of course. She continued to sit cross-legged on the floor, looking up at man and boy sitting side by side on the toddler bed, yearning for something she never wanted to want.

John-Parker Wisdom, the man she'd planned to dislike, to reject, was getting to her without even trying.

# *Chapter Ten*

They tiptoed down the stairs together, comfortable in the cozy, mellow mood the story time had created.

When they reached the bottom, far enough away not to disturb the children, John-Parker said, "I found something in the attic I'd like to show you."

Zoey smiled. "Another broken tennis racket? Or one-legged chair? Exciting."

They had found some interesting but useless items in the house. And John-Parker had barely begun exploring the attic space.

"Letters. Papers. Come on up. I'll show you. Maybe you'll understand what they mean."

"You're being mysterious, and I'm intrigued." So she followed him to the pull-down stairs and climbed up and into the large open space at the top of the house.

They'd expected the attic to house heating and air ducts and not much else. The surprise was a jumble of dust-covered junk, trunks, boxes and tattered furniture strewn over the plywood floor. The accumulation of many, many years that neither John-Parker nor Zoey had ever heard mentioned.

From the ceiling, a single, bare light bulb dangled to illuminate the area.

She was glad he'd left the light on.

John-Parker came up behind her and went directly to a dusty old suitcase.

"Sorry about the dust. Your clothes will be covered."

She shrugged away the comment. "What's the mystery?"

He gave her an odd glance she didn't understand and opened a large suitcase of papers and letters.

"We've found lots of old documents in the house," she said. "What's special about these?"

"They're…puzzling. Everything else we've found makes sense. These don't. Well, some do, but I didn't know…" He shook his head as if aware his rambling made little sense to her. "You'll see."

Curious, Zoey tugged a half-full paint bucket close to the battered antique luggage.

John-Parker handed her a packet of letters from the top of a considerable stack. "I haven't sorted through everything yet, but read these."

By the end of the third letter, she looked up at him, shocked and bewildered. "These are to Mamie from her husband."

A husband she'd never mentioned.

"Didn't you know she was married?"

"No. She never talked about her life before Rosemary Ridge. Like everyone else, I assumed she'd never been married and that was the reason she took in foster kids—to create the family she wanted."

"Yeah, well, wait until you read the rest of those. Prepare to be bewildered."

Even more curious now, Zoey started to lay aside the letter to read the next one, but John-Parker stopped her. "Look at his signature."

"'Love you to eternity and beyond, Brian.'" She gasped. "Brian. The name she spoke shortly before her death. Her husband was named Brian. Why didn't she ever talk about him?"

"I wondered the same. Apparently, something happened to their marriage."

"Divorce." The bitterness rose in her throat. "He probably cheated, broke their vows, and forgot all about his 'eternity and beyond' promises."

She thrust the letter back in the envelope, suddenly angry for the woman who'd given so much to so many and yet had been betrayed by the man who'd claimed to love her.

John-Parker caught her hand. "We don't know that. You're jumping to conclusions."

She dashed a hand across a tickle on her cheek, stunned to realize the tickle was a tear.

"Hey. Hey." John-Parker shifted closer until he could wrap an arm around her shoulders and give her a kindly squeeze. "Want to talk about it?"

"Cheating husbands?" She huffed, aware of the bitterness in her words. "I know all about them. Men cheat. That's what I know."

"Not every man."

"Tell that to Owen and Olivia when they get big enough to ask about their father and how he died."

"How did he die?"

"I'm too ashamed to tell you." She couldn't look him in the eye, but nevertheless found herself leaning into his strength, glad for his quiet acceptance of her uncharacteristic outburst. She hadn't leaned on a man in years. Instead of feeling weak and helpless, Zoey felt comforted.

"His sin is not on you, Zoey. Your husband cheated. His choices are not your fault."

"According to Vic, they were. If I was a better wife…" Her voice choked, drifting away in the memory of inadequacy. "Our friends knew he cheated and no one said a word. How's that for real friends?" Acid laced her tone. "He humiliated me at every turn. Even in death."

"I'm sorry."

"You know the real kicker? His girlfriend was with him in that boating accident, wearing an engagement ring he bought on *our* credit. All of the ugliness came out in the newspapers and on social media. *I* had to pay for *her* ring." The first of many debts he'd left behind for her to square.

Eventually, she'd sold the ring, but the horrible reminder of Vic's betrayal hadn't even brought enough to pay for his funeral, much less the huge amounts Vic had charged to their credit card.

Tears clogged Zoey's throat, infuriating her. "I don't cry. This is stupid."

"Maybe you need to." He shifted until her cheek was against his chest and his powerful arms snuggled her close. Beneath his button-down shirt, his heart beat, steady, strong, reassuring.

Zoey knew she should move away. Hadn't she promised never to let another man get close enough to hurt her or her kids?

Instead, she rested for long, quiet seconds, dust and manly cologne filling her nostrils as she accepted his comfort.

She'd been wrong about John-Parker Wisdom, although she still couldn't reconcile his fifteen-year absence with the man she'd come to know. A strong, determined man who showed tenderness to her kids and kindness to her. A friend, a fun guy, a smart co-worker. And more.

She closed her eyes and wished she could remain in John-Parker's arms forever.

Was she falling prey to another charming man who'd ultimately hurt her?

She was very afraid she was.

For the sake of her children, she must keep her heart out of the situation.

Slowly, reluctantly, she untangled herself from John-Parker, aware that she'd snuggled into him like a lonely child.

He seemed to hold on as if he, too, was reluctant to separate them.

That wouldn't do at all.

"I shouldn't have done that," she said, frustrated to wish he still held her.

"We all need a shoulder now and then." His tone was casual and steady, as if he was not at all affected by the moment. Not like she was.

Foolish woman. So needy.

Stiffening her resolve, she dashed away the remnant of those ridiculous tears. "Even you?"

"Sure."

He didn't elaborate and she didn't push, but she could not imagine the confident bodyguard leaning on anyone.

"Well." She forced a self-conscious laugh. "If you ever need a shoulder, mine isn't very big, but it's available."

Even footing. He'd comforted her. She'd comfort him. Tit for tat and no strings attached.

John-Parker's stormy eyes met hers. A bare smile tipped the corners of his lips. "I'll remember that."

She reached for another packet of letters, eager to do something besides make a fool of herself.

Heat ran along the back of John-Parker's neck, down his arms and across his chest where he'd touched Zoey. He'd gone from feeling sorry for her because of her louse of a husband to feeling something far more disturbing.

He liked holding her. Even now, he wanted to pull her back into his arms, hold her close to his heart.

The Myrick brothers were right.

He liked her. A lot. Found her attractive in ways he hadn't expected. The way she loved her children. Her concern for the homeless. The woman hit the floor running each morning and never slowed down until long after he left for the night.

Now, she sat on the rickety old paint bucket, head down, embarrassed by the past few minutes. She shouldn't be. She'd done nothing wrong. Nor had he.

He wanted her to realize that good men existed who didn't cheat. If he ever found the right woman who could endure his work absences and dangerous lifestyle, he'd treat her like a precious jewel. He sure wouldn't go looking for anyone else.

Zoey needed to experience that kind of man in her life.

The notion caught him up short. What was he thinking? That he was some superhero swooping in to save the day the way he did in his business?

Couldn't happen. He'd show her kindness, try to convince her that Jesus was more than a popular curse word, and compromise with her on Mamie's house—a little—but that's where he stopped. Had to.

No matter how much the man in him wanted to erase the pain in saw her eyes.

Those pain-filled eyes glanced up from the letters and caught him staring. Heat crested her cheekbones.

"Don't judge me," she said.

"I'm not." Not even close, but apparently she expected censure instead of admiration. To break his troubled thoughts, he motioned toward the letters on her lap.

"Find anything else interesting?"

"Mamie and her husband seemed to love each other. He misses her, longs to see her beautiful face, reads and rereads every letter she sends." A wistful smile lifted Zoey's lips. "The words are so private and personal, I feel intrusive reading them."

"We both lived with her. Yet we weren't aware of someone as fundamentally important as a husband. I never heard anything about her past life, did you?"

"Now that I think about it, no."

"Don't you wonder why she never told us?"

"You think the other letters could give us answers?" She ran her fingers over the aged letters, expression pensive. "Does her past even matter now?"

"It matters to me. She matters. I thought I knew her before. After the unexpected will and now this letter, I realize we may not have known her at all."

"But why is that important now, John-Parker? She's gone."

"Lots of reasons." Guilt. The need to honor Mamie in ways that assuaged his conscience. Curiosity. A deep desire to know the woman who'd never forgotten him.

There lay the puzzle he couldn't stop thinking about. "Mainly, I'm hoping the letters or something we find in all these papers explains why she included me in her will."

He'd come to understand why Zoey was an heir. Mamie had loved her niece and those two little ones. She'd wanted to provide for them. He, on the other hand, was the outlier. Or, as some in this town thought, the outlaw.

Regardless, John-Parker Wisdom was a fighter, unable and unwilling to back down from a conviction. He strongly believed he was meant to create a sanctuary in this house for lost boys. Somehow. Mamie would want him to forge ahead.

If only he could find something in her Bible, her journal, or in these letters to convince his naysayers. Including Zoey.

For the next ten minutes, they read in silence, sorting the letters by date. Suddenly, his eyes blurred. He reread the words. Read them a third time.

"Zoey," he said, tone incredulous.

Putting a finger to hold her place, she looked up, shook back her dark brown waves. He recalled the soft silk of her hair against his hand and his chin when she'd burrowed into his chest and let him hold her.

"Did you find something?"

He dragged his thoughts back to the shocking letter. A letter that made Mamie more of a mystery than he'd ever imagined.

"More than something." He held the yellowed page out for her to see. "Mamie and Brian had a child."

"What?" Zoey jerked upright and nearly tipped the bucket over. "No way. Mamie would have told me."

She took the letter and read for herself.

"He says he can't wait to see her and their new son." She glanced up, blinked a few times to be sure she wasn't imagining things, and then read again. "She had a baby. John-Parker. A son."

The light of understanding flashed in John-Parker's eyes. He pointed at her. "Remember the kid's book we found with the inscription from Mommy to Brian?"

"Oh, my. John-Parker. The book must have belonged to her son." Zoey pressed the letter against her heart, the mother in her connecting with Mamie in a new way. "No wonder she kept it even though the pages were nearly gone."

A scowl darkened John-Parker's expression. "Are you telling me no one in your family knew Mamie had a child? She was your aunt. Why didn't you know any of this?"

Zoey drew in a breath, held it, her cheeks puffed out in consternation. Time for full disclosure.

"She wasn't really my aunt."

He bristled. "So you lied?"

"'Aunt' was a term of endearment for a woman I loved very much, John-Parker. I considered her a relative, whether blood was involved or not. She and my grandmother, who raised me, knew each other and…" The fire in John-Parker's expression stopped the flow of words. She finished with a weak, pitiful apology. "I never meant to mislead you."

He stared at her so long, her temper started to rise.

Why should she have to explain? And who was he to pass judgement after what he'd done? Or better yet, not done, for Mamie.

John-Parker's nostrils flared. "Hard to believe, especially since your inheritance is at stake."

"That's not fair. I did nothing wrong, no matter what you think." Incensed, she placed the bundle of letters back in the suitcase and rose.

A few minutes ago, they'd been friends, partners, and she'd had tender thoughts about him.

Which showed what a fool a woman could be when a man gave her the least bit of attention.

She didn't need him or his high horse.

Except, she did. Because of the house. Because of Aunt Mamie, a woman more mysterious and complex than either of them had imagined.

But right now she was too angry and hurt to figure out the past. The present pressed too heavily.

He'd upset her. Angered her.

He did not, he realized, want her to be mad at him.

John-Parker sat on the broken attic chair alternately reading letters and thinking about the complicated woman who'd stormed down the stairs so fast he'd held his breath, thinking she'd fall.

The bodyguard in him never took a day off.

With a huff, he muttered, "Probably accuse me of pushing her if she fell and I intervened."

Like Mamie and this house, Zoey Chavez was full of surprises. He'd wondered how she and Mamie were kin. Now he knew the truth. They weren't. Like him, she had no real claim on Mamie Bezek.

Yet, here they were, two unrelated strangers, fighting over a gift from Mamie.

Rubbing a hand over his tired eyes, John-Parker struggled to find the balance.

"Lord, I want to do the right thing, but Zoey confuses the situation. What am I to do about her?"

And those kids. Owen and Olivia had wiggled into his heart even if their mother disliked him.

But did she? He didn't think so. This house and Mamie's will had become both common ground and battleground.

What was the answer?

*Get along with everyone as much as possible. How you react is up to you.* Isn't that what the Bible said? And what Mamie tried to drill into his hard head? Yet, Zoey was the guilty party. She'd lied, regardless of her excuses.

On the other hand, he was the Christian. Even if he had some arbitrary "right" to be angry, scripture took precedence. Forgive and make peace.

He just hadn't expected peace with Zoey to take so much effort.

One minute, they were partners enjoying the remodel process and the discovery of these letters. In the next, he was left alone in the stuffy attic with piles of junk, a dusty old suitcase full of letters, and the nagging feeling that he'd done something wrong.

John-Parker sighed so hard the letter in his hand fluttered. He folded the single sheet back into the envelope.

In his business dealings with employees and clients, he'd learned that facing issues head-on in a calm manner was the best way to handle disagreements. Clear the air, find a solution, move forward.

Was there an agreeable solution to Zoey Chavez?

He found her in the kitchen, banging pots and pans into the bottom of the stove.

"Can we talk?"

"Go away." She slammed the oven bottom, her back to him.

He touched her shoulder. "I shouldn't have called you a liar."

"No, you shouldn't have. Now, leave me alone so I can do my work."

He took the pot from her hand. "Let me help."

Mouth tight, she shot him a flaming glare. "It's getting late. I'm going to bed."

"The Bible says not to go to bed angry. You'll wake up worse off than ever."

"Don't spout your Bible to me." She yanked the pan from him.

"Have to." He took the pan back. "God's pecking on my conscience because I hurt your feelings. If I was wrong, and I think I was, I'm sorry."

"If God told you that, He was right."

"He always is. I'm the one who messed up, not Him."

"Okay. Apology accepted." Finally standing still, she gnawed at one corner of her mouth. "Maybe I should have explained my relationship with Mamie more fully."

"I probably wouldn't have listened at first."

In an eye-rolling, I-give-up gesture, she lowered one hip and shoulder. "You're really good at eating crow, you know that?" Then, as if she'd realized how friendly she sounded, she squinted at him. "Or are you trying to manipulate me into liking you again?"

Did that mean she'd liked him before? Nice.

He raised both eyebrows and did his best to look innocent. "Is it working?"

A glint of humor flashed in brown irises. "Maybe. I don't like being mad at anyone, even you. Want some tea or coffee?"

He wasn't fond of anger himself. He was, however, fond of her.

"Can we have milk and cookies instead?" John-Parker asked, more as conciliation than hunger. Besides, he rarely got homemade cookies and hers were good. A win-win in his book.

The humor in her eyes intensified. "Your sweet tooth's showing."

"Can't help it. You make the best."

"Oh, now you're working it."

She was right. He was.

The ups and downs with Zoey were making him a little nutty, but he had to admit he enjoyed the ups. Like him, she had a hard time staying mad. He liked that quality in a woman.

Feeling better already, he went to the now-doorless pantry and removed a Ziploc of Zoey's homemade chocolate-chip cookies. As with the cabinet doors, the outdated pantry door had been removed and sent to the cabinetmaker's for refacing. Refreshing instead of replacing the solid oak cabinets would save thousands of dollars they could use on the outdoor facility he wanted for the boys. *If* he found a way to get around Earl Beck and his nuisance law.

"For the record," he said easily, handing her the cookie bag, "I like you, too."

Their eyes locked. He knew that look. Had seen it in a frightened client. Panic.

He reached out to reassure her, but she moved away.

She could say she liked him yet he wasn't allowed to return the compliment?

Recalling the disaster with her husband, he tried to understand. She was afraid of falling in love again.

He stopped right there and did a U-turn.

He liked her. He couldn't love her.

Cautious now for both of them, John-Parker turned the topic back to their attic discoveries.

"I can't stop thinking about Mamie's letters." That much was true, even if the tiff with Zoey still bothered him. "Why did she keep her past hidden?"

"She must have had a reason."

"You knew her better than I ever did." And treated her better.

"Apparently not as well as I thought. Now I realize how much I took and how little I gave."

He could relate to that. He'd done nothing for Mamie. He'd only taken.

Sorrow drilled a hole in his soul as he found two glasses and set them on the table. The guilt of his misspent youth and the fifteen-year absence weighed on him like a pickup truck.

He'd accused Zoey of taking advantage of Mamie when, in fact, she'd been the better person.

"You were here for her," he said, painfully aware that he had not been. "You took care of her when she was sick."

Zoey shook her head, her expression as sad as he felt. "Wasn't enough. Even after she got sick, she focused on the kids and me. She'd order clothes for us online, but never for herself. Once, I tried to force the issue after a surprise box arrived for me and the kids. Mamie broke my heart with her response." She looked at him with glassy eyes. "She was dying, she'd said, what was the point?"

Grief stabbed John-Parker through the chest. He almost spouted tears.

"Yeah," he said around the thick knot of emotion. "That was Mamie. She'd claim that her old shoes were too comfortable to give up when they were obviously worn out. Stuff like that happened all the time. Always for us, never for her. If we were short on fried chicken, guess who suddenly went on a diet and wanted only salad?" He shook his head. "Why couldn't I see that back then?"

Zoey touched his shoulder. "John-Parker, you were only a boy."

Her compassion tightened the knot in his throat. Or maybe learning that his failure was greater than he'd realized choked him.

"We were a bunch of self-focused kids caring only about ourselves." He'd stolen from Mamie, abandoned her, and yet she'd never stopped loving him.

Like Jesus.

The piercing poignance of such love made him want to be a better man. And that was the whole point of remodeling this house, to build a bigger, better, home for teenage boys. If he continued Mamie's legacy of love and giving, maybe he'd feel the forgiveness he needed so badly.

If only for this reason, he couldn't allow anyone to stop him. Not the council, and not even Zoey, no matter how much he liked her. He had to find a way to make the foster home happen.

Zoey put a hand on his arm. "You're here now," she said, "trying to do a good thing. Don't be too hard on yourself."

Compassion from Zoey touched him in ways he couldn't explain. He met her warm, brown gaze and held on.

The undefinable *thing* between them sprang up and hovered in the room; a soft blanket, a yearning. Competitors, friends, co-heirs. What were they?

He wrapped his fingers over hers, holding her touch against him, feeling the warmth of her skin through his shirt.

Zoey was as complex as their benefactress.

Something deep and unsettling, but sweet, too, shifted between them. That hovering *thing.*

He couldn't name it—didn't want to—but he definitely felt the change.

"Be careful." He kept his voice light with gentle humor and did his best to steer away from his wayward thoughts. "You're getting soft on me. Next thing you know, you'll agree with all my most excellent plans and storm city hall on my behalf."

With a snort that was half serious, half amused, she pulled her hand away and sat back.

"Don't kid yourself."

"Aw, now. I thought the boys and my fantastic ideas were growing on you."

She arched an eyebrow at him. "Just because I feel sorry for River and Charlie does not mean I've changed my mind."

"You still think they're bad kids?"

"I didn't say that, John-Parker. I like them, although River can get on my last nerve sometimes."

"He's got a lot of good in him."

"Agreed. So, don't think I'm a hard case because I want to sell this house. I care about those kids, but my kids come first."

"Understandable." He got that. He really did. But wasn't there a way to serve the best interests of both? He was still ruminating on that.

"Charlie's a sweet kid." She lay a cookie on half a paper towel. "He plays Legos with Owen sometimes."

"Thanks for letting him."

She hitched a shoulder. "No big deal."

Although John-Parker recalled how adamant she'd been about keeping *those boys* away from her children, he didn't say so. "It's a big deal to Charlie. And me."

Her dark eyes flashed to his. Again, he felt that odd shift.

"I'm human, John-Parker," she said softly, "whether you believe me or not."

"Oh, I believe you," John-Parker replied, his own voice surprisingly hushed and tender. "Lately, more than I want to."

She stared at him for long beats of time while he tried to figure out his own meaning.

Then, as if she desperately wanted to change the mood in the room, she turned away and hurried to the fridge.

Tension sprang up where tenderness had been.

Hers. His.

"Milk," she muttered. "We forgot the milk."

Was she feeling something more than competition for him? Was she, like him, fighting an attraction neither could afford to feel?

She turned from the fridge, milk jug aloft. “Ever since we discovered that Mamie and Brian had a child, I can’t get that off my mind. That’s a big deal. Where are Brian and their son? Why is her son not in the will, but you and I are? Why did she give her entire life to sacrificially raise someone else’s children?”

So many questions neither of them could answer.

“I came back to give her everything,” he mused. “But she’d already had everything she’d wanted and had somehow lost them.”

“Family.”

“Even if she and Brian separated for some reason, where is her son?”

“I’m as puzzled as you are. The letters were sent to an address in Nashville. Could he or Brian still live there?”

“If so, why weren’t they here with her? Why is neither, especially the son, listed in the will?” He reached for another cookie, though he didn’t remember tasting the first one. “I didn’t even know she’d lived in Tennessee.”

To a kid, Mamie Bezek began and ended in this town, especially in this house. He’d never bothered to know more about her.

“I guess I knew but hadn’t thought about it. When they were young, she and my grandma attended Belmont University together. That’s where they became friends.”

“Did you ever visit her in Tennessee?”

“No. By the time I came along, Grandma was in Omaha and Mamie lived here in Rosemary Ridge.”

“Without a husband or son.”

“Which can only mean one of two things.” Zoey turned sad eyes on him. “Either they had a terrible estrangement or—”

John-Parker finished her sentence. “They died.”

# Chapter Eleven

Late into the night, long after cookies and milk had been cleared away and John-Parker had returned to his rental, Zoey sat cross-legged on her bed, laptop open, searching for answers.

As someone who worked a part-time job through her computer, she knew how to research. Before morning, she'd sent a handful of compelling, heartbreaking documents to her printer.

With the news swirling in her mind, she'd slept little. At daylight, she'd texted John-Parker, urging him to stop by as soon as he could.

He'd texted back a long list of errands on his agenda but promised to head her way in ten minutes.

In the meantime, workmen arrived and roamed up and down the basement stairs with equipment and drywall.

A thrill ran through Zoey at the rapid progress. They'd promised what sounded impossible. To have the basement ready for the move within a week.

By the time John-Parker arrived, Zoey had Olivia in her high chair destroying a bowl of Cheerios and Owen at the table eating with much more finesse.

"What's up?"

"I found something." She motioned toward a file folder on the table. "Want coffee?"

"I'll get it. Tell me what you discovered. Something in the other letters?"

He went to the soon-to-be demolished counter and poured two cups of coffee, lacing hers with caramel creamer and his with sugar. He never failed to notice little details like her drink preferences.

"On the computer. I did a records search for Mamie in Tennessee."

She didn't mention the quick search she'd also done on his business and had come away impressed.

"You must have stayed up late." He paused in stirring the mugs to squint at her. "No wonder you look exhausted."

"Thank you for the compliment. Exactly what every woman likes to hear."

He grinned. "Only you can look pretty and tired at the same time."

She made a face at him, amused, as usual, by his easy ways. "Sneaky. Now I can't be mad at you."

If she let them, his compliments could turn her head. She needed to remember that he was only temporarily in her life. If anything, her research of his business emphasized that truth. She could like him but she had to guard her heart from anything more.

He handed her the coffee. "Show me these documents."

After saving Olivia's bowl from an accidental tumble to the floor, Zoey opened the folder on the table. John-Parker took the bench seat next to Owen, who poked bites of banana into his mouth and looked up at John-Parker with an adoring gaze.

After patting the boy on the back and reminding him to chew before he swallowed, John-Parker alternately sipped his coffee and thumbed through the pages. When his stomach growled, Owen offered him a bite of banana.

He took a pinch. A tiny bite that pleased her son no end. "I shared, Mom."

Zoey's heart squeezed as she observed the tender, fatherly interplay between the big man and her small son.

Would John-Parker's departure sadden her little boy? Would he feel rejected, abandoned? She'd seen the results of rejection in River and Charlie and wanted to protect her son from that kind of hurt.

But how?

The worry clung to her like static on a cold, dry morning, crackling to life at the slightest kindness John-Parker showed to Owen. And to her.

"Thank you, Owen," she managed to say around the lump in her throat as she transferred Olivia from her high chair to the floor. "If you're finished, go play with Olivia while John-Parker and I discuss something important."

Though his expression said he'd rather be with John-Parker, Owen reluctantly complied.

As he finished reading the final page, John-Parker squeezed his lip between thumb and finger, a habit she'd noticed many times when he was deep in thought.

Finally, his tone heavy, he said, "Her entire family gone in a car wreck."

The information was all in the folder. Mamie's marriage certificate to Brian Bezek. The birth of not one but two sons and, tragically, the death certificates for all three. The boys had only been nine and eleven.

Zoey had even discovered the newspaper clippings about the accident and the settlement Mamie had received from the drunk driver's insurance. A significant amount that she must have used to buy this property and make investments that now belonged to her and John-Parker.

For the hundredth time, Zoey wished Mamie had spent that money on herself.

Heart sore, Zoey eased into Owen's place, next to John-Parker. "According to the newspaper article, Mamie wasn't with them. She'd been sick that day, at home with the flu, when Brian took the boys out for pizza."

"Tragic."

"After that, I find her here in Rosemary Ridge, when she bought this house."

"I wonder why she came here?"

"Probably the same reason anyone moves away after heartbreak. The same reason I accepted her generous offer. To leave the painful memories behind."

"Maybe that's why she never talked about her family. The grief was too overwhelming. She kept their memories alive in that suitcase in the attic."

"Where she never visited."

"That we know of."

Zoey understood as only a mother could. "Losing my children would destroy me. I don't know how Mamie kept on breathing."

John-Parker rubbed the top of her hand. "People grieve in different ways. Some become bitter and mad at God and the world. Some choose to make the world better. Mamie took her grief and her insurance settlement and turned them into hope for others."

"All those years, she carried so much pain. Yet she kept on smiling."

"Always. Did you notice the eleven-year old's name?"

Zoey nodded. She had. "Brian Bezek, Junior. Now we know for sure the book we found belonged to Mamie's little boy, a gift from her on his third birthday."

"She kept it all these years, tatters and all."

"That breaks my heart."

"Mine, too." The ache in his voice echoed the one in her soul. She leaned her head against his shoulder, both giving and taking comfort.

He drew her in, placing a hand on her cheek, a simple gesture that said so much.

No one had comforted her in a long time and now John-Parker had done so twice in as many days. She didn't move away. Refused to listen to the warning voice in her head. She needed this, needed him. No one else could understand the way he could.

"Do you think," he ask, his breath warm against her hair, "that her sons are the reason she favored boys and gave the rest of her life to care for them? For us?"

He stroked the side of her face, sending shivers through her. Every cell in her body wanted to stay there forever. With him. Forget their disagreements. Forget the sadness they'd discovered in the attic. Focus on each other and the attraction that grew like dandelion weeds in Mamie's yard.

Not good. Not good at all.

Zoey straightened and moved slightly away. She couldn't

quite look at him yet, not without revealing the emotion he'd see in her eyes.

*Stay strong, Zoey,* she reminded herself. *Focus on the kids, the house, Mamie. Forget John-Parker.*

She'd have to soon enough. Might as well start now.

"One of her favorite sayings was when life gives you lemons make lemonade," John-Parker said, apparently not nearly as affected by her as she was by him.

"She did that, didn't she?" Was her face red? Her cheeks burned. Did he notice?

"Your research answers a lot of questions."

"Except one big one."

"Yes. You and me." He got that troubled look again, the one that made her want to comfort him. "Why are we her main heirs? Why me, in particular?"

She squeezed the top of his hand. "I'll keep digging."

"There may be more answers in the attic. Or maybe in her journal."

"I wonder if her attorney knows anything more."

"Our next progress check-in is next Tuesday. We'll find out." He glanced at his smartwatch. "Gotta run. I have an appointment."

She wanted to ask but didn't. None of her business where he went or what he did, as long he adhered to the will's requirements. Yet she knew she'd miss him the minute he drove away.

Her heart was giving her serious problems when it came to stubborn, aggravating, kind and warmhearted John-Parker Wisdom. Confusing—that's what he was. And a man who held a woman with tenderness and asked nothing in return.

After putting his coffee cup in the sink, John-Parker stepped into the living room. She heard his low tones as he spoke to the kids. Curious, she followed and saw Olivia stretch her tiny arms up to him. He crouched for a hug in the same moment that Owen slammed into him from the other side. With a laugh, John-Parker tumbled sideways, landing off-balance on his left hip. Somehow, both kids were cradled safely in his protective arms.

The way she'd wanted to be a few minutes ago.

She pressed a palm to her cheek, felt the residual warmth, and hoped John-Parker didn't notice.

Owen giggled. "Again, John-Parker. Do it again. Throw me higher."

John-Parker untangled himself and stood, lifting Olivia first and flying her slowly over his head in a gentle airplane motion.

"Me, John-Parker, me." Owen hopped up and down, begging for attention. Zoey hurt for her son.

John-Parker obliged, soaring her son whose short arms outstretched to imitate a plane with increased gusto. The toddler's laughter echoed through the house.

Her babies were falling for him. Like their foolish mama.

Zoey's heart thudded heavily as she watched and listened, her head leaned against the doorjamb. Her kids were happy, delighted at the attention. Though she and her friends played with them, she'd never allowed a man her age to enter their lives.

She shouldn't have allowed it with John-Parker.

But she could not deny them—or herself—these moments of happiness.

In only a few weeks, he'd be gone, out of her life, the final decisions made.

As much as she wanted the issues of the house and will resolved for good, saying goodbye to John-Parker would be harder than she'd imagined.

As he settled the children back on the rug with their toys, promising to stop by later with River and Charlie, he spotted her.

She hoped he thought she was watching her children, not him.

"How about Chinese take-out tonight when the boys come over? I'll bring ice cream, too, in case you want dessert."

There he went again. Making her happy and sad at the

same time. "Chinese sounds amazing. I won't have to cook." She pushed at his chest, teasing. "And you're buying."

He captured her hand against his heart, an action she liked too much. "Thanks for doing that research. I know you're tired. I'll get back here ASAP so you can take a nap with the tots while I help the guys on your new living quarters."

"Stop being nice. We're still selling this house." Except, her protests grew weaker all the time. John-Parker wanted to do something special here, the way Mamie had. Now that she knew about her aunt's past, she was starting to want that, too.

Except she couldn't. Her kids' futures rested with this house, didn't they?

"Hey." John-Parker moved a step closer. "Why the frown?"

"As you said, tired." That much was true in more than one way. She was tired, all right. Tired of worrying about the house, her future, her children, her growing feelings for John-Parker. Mostly, she was tired of being afraid all the time.

Just when she decided she couldn't handle another thing to worry about, John-Parker leaned in and kissed her on the forehead.

"Hang in there, pretty mama. I won't let anything bad happen to you or those kids."

Why had he kissed her? Why had he made a promise he couldn't keep? At least, not for long.

John-Parker couldn't get the questions out of his mind as he headed for what had become a semiregular breakfast with Wink, Frank and whoever else happened to join them. The old guys were godly men, full of wisdom, wit, and they'd introduced or reintroduced John-Parker to half the town. As a result, more and more people spoke approvingly of the project they'd begun calling "Mamie's House of Hope."

He liked that title. Maybe he'd keep it. Much better than Mamie's street rats. Maybe he'd order a giant sign for the front yard. Or not. He wanted the boys who lived there to feel at home, not institutionalized.

But what to do about Zoey? He couldn't leave her high and dry, not now, when he'd come to know and respect, even admire, her.

Fact was, she attracted him as no woman had in years. And those children. For a man with no prior interest in hearth and home, they'd snuggled right under his heart and stayed there.

He couldn't let them down. They stirred his protective instincts to a higher level than he'd thought possible, given his occupation. A level of love as well as duty.

He made his way through the usual gaggle of humanity inside the Drugstore Café, his nostrils filled with warm breakfast scents, and settled with yet another cup of hot brew. Wink, Frank and the two local veterinarians, Jake Colter and old Doc Howell, were deep in conversation about one of Wink's sick calves.

John-Parker only half listened, his mind on Zoey and his uncharacteristic impulsiveness. He was a man who planned every detail. He kept a running schedule on his phone, along with a calendar, a spreadsheet and a to-do list. Kissing Zoey and making macho promises was not on his agenda.

"Wink and Frank told us about the trouble you had at the last town council." Dr. Colter's words brought him out of his reverie.

"Yep. He-he." Chuckling with ornery delight, Wink reached for his coffee. "Old Earl Beck sure got his knickers in a knot."

"Ain't nothing new about that." Frank's beefy hands scraped grape jelly onto a piece of toast. "Beck's been in a foul mood since his wife left him for that tortilla salesman."

"Any more news on the whole nuisance ordinance thing?" Wink asked. "A lot of nonsense, if you ask me. Hogs, my eye."

Setting his coffee down, John-Parker shook his head. "I'm going to ask for a special meeting and try again."

"I know Earl pretty well," Dr. Howell said around his gray mustache. "Maybe I could have a talk with him."

"Earl is the big mouth of the group." Wink waved his butter knife like a baton. "If he'd shut his trap, I think you'd be in like Flint or whoever that feller was."

"Beck has his reasons for disliking me," John-Parker said.

"Oh, I know that, son. I've done animal doctoring in this town for forty-plus years. Some of Mamie's boys were ornery."

"Worse than ornery, and that's what the council is worried about. I can't blame them for that, but those boys need a home and training with people who care enough to direct them and give them a better future. If we don't help them, they lose and society loses."

"You won't hear me disagree." Doc took a bite of gravy-soaked biscuit.

"Me neither." Frank pointed a crisp piece of bacon. "Wouldn't hurt for you to talk to the council again. Ask for that special session and come prepared with all the statistic mumbo-jumbo people spout to prove their point."

"Brother is right." Wink broke off a dainty piece of muffin. "Talk to Mayor Ben. He's a reasonable man. That's why he's mayor. He'll hear you."

John-Parker tilted his head at the old cowboy. "You been talking to him for me?"

Frank huffed. "John-Parker, you ought to know by now, Wink can't keep his snout out of anything."

"Neither can you," Wink said amiably. "But that's not the point here. I'm trying to help John-Parker and those boys."

"You think I'm not? Any man who eats meatloaf and fried eggs and wants to better this town is a friend of mine."

John-Parker suppressed a grin at the bickering brothers. "Some people see me as worsening the town, Frank. Including Zoey."

Frank propped an elbow on the tabletop and squinted at John-Parker. "There you go, talking about Zoey."

Wink snorted. "She's pretty and she's single. He'd be blind if he didn't notice her."

That much was true, not that John-Parker wanted to admit it. "Like I told you before, she wants to sell the house outright. I understand her need for the money, but—"

"But you feel led to care for teenage boys the way Mamie did."

"In here—" John-Parker thumped a fist against his left chest "—I know reopening Mamie's house as a real home for boys is the right thing to do."

"Uh-huh." Frank nodded. "You've got a calling."

He'd never consider the desire a calling but, yes, maybe so. Didn't he believe God was guiding, even orchestrating, this trip to Rosemary Ridge?

"But how do I reconcile my goal with Zoey's? I don't want to cause a problem for her or her kids."

There was the thing that kept him up at night. Finding a way around the town council and their nuisance clause was possible. But Zoey and those kids presented a problem he couldn't solve.

"We been thinking about that," Wink said. "Praying, too. There's more than one way around a standoff."

The old guys prayed for him? He'd take that anytime. "I'm listening."

"Why not ask Zoey to stay on as the boss lady?" the cowboy asked.

Frank scoffed, digging an elbow into his brother's ribs. "Pretty young woman like Zoey with a bunch of teenage boys? Bad idea, brother. I done told you that."

Wink ruffled up like a bantam rooster. "Mamie did it alone. Zoey could have her own private quarters if she wanted. From what I've seen of her with the homeless folks, she's tough and fearless but kindhearted, too. After the way she looked after Mamie, I think she could do about anything."

The idea wasn't terrible. Zoey could make the basement apartment her permanent quarters and never have to move again. But would she agree?

"You think about it, son." Wink patted him on the shoulder. "Wouldn't hurt to ask. If all else fails, we got us another idea."

"Won't hurt to talk to Mayor Ben again, either, see what he's learned about the legalities. He's at the fire station this morning. I saw his Jeep." Frank propped his elbow on the table and crooked a beefy finger toward John-Parker. "One other thing to put under your hat and consider. Sometimes asking for forgiveness or offering recompense goes a long ways."

Although he wasn't sure what Frank meant, John-Parker nodded as he crunched into a strip of crispy bacon.

He couldn't ask Mamie for the forgiveness he desperately wanted, but he was doing his best to redeem himself by continuing her legacy in the house. Was that the recompense Frank meant?

While John-Parker continued to eat and ponder, Dr. Howell pushed back his emptied plate. "Got to get to work, so I can take off early. Helen wants to go fishing." He grinned, clearly pleased that his frequently ill wife felt well enough for an outing. "I'll give Earl a call, John-Parker, see what I can do to help out." To the other vet, he said, "Jake, don't rush. I see your pretty wife getting out of her car, heading this way."

Dr. Jake Colter put down his fork and rose, his expression brightening. "Save my plate, fellas. Rachel's here." He started toward the door.

John-Parker, sitting on the side facing the entrance, couldn't help noticing the couple.

Colter's dark-haired wife stepped into the café. When she saw her husband, a smile of pure joy broke over her face. Joy and love and pleasure to see her man when they'd likely been together at home only a short time ago.

*Every separation must feel like forever when you love that much.*

A pinch of envy surprised John-Parker.

He'd been alone and too busy for such a long time that he'd put aside romantic thoughts. But since arriving in Rosemary Ridge, they were back, tormenting him with questions.

Would he ever find joy in coming home to a wife? Children? Would a woman ever miss him, love him, that much?

# *Chapter Twelve*

Zoey tried to focus on work, the kids, the hundred and one things left to do before the house could be put on the market. She tried, but John-Parker's unexpected kiss crowded in, tender and sweet.

This morning, before the summer heat had time to drive her inside, she'd given up working on anything that required concentration and had taken the children into the garden. When she moved from this house, the canned and frozen vegetables would move with her. A farmers market this weekend meant extra cash as well. And a garden did not maintain itself.

Add to that the racket inside the house, and outdoors was the only place to be. Hammers banged. Nail guns popped. Saws buzzed a high pitch loud enough to drive anyone away. Progress was noisy.

So why couldn't she drop the topic of John-Parker and that tiny touch of his warm, firm lips to her forehead.

"I'm making a mountain out of a molehill," she muttered. Like some geeky high-school girl with a crush on the star quarterback.

"What, Mom?" Owen, scanning the trellised tomato vines for red-ripe fruit, stopped to look at her.

"Nothing, baby."

"Are you praying? John-Parker prays. He said God listens always."

Did He? She found that hard to believe, although she'd started wishing it was true. Wishing and sometimes even tossing up a prayer to test her theory.

"Did you find a tomato?" She refused to dwell on God or John-Parker.

"Two!" With the easy distraction of a three-year-old, Owen happily carried the almost-ripe tomatoes to the basket.

She bent to hug her son and almost kissed his forehead. Probably because that's where her thoughts were this morning. Kisses and foreheads.

John-Parker had kissed her the way she kissed her babies. He hadn't meant anything serious by it. Friendship. Kindness.

Except, she knew better. This *thing* between her and John-Parker buzzed louder every time they were together. Every single day. Her fingertips touched her forehead, feeling the warmth and emotion all over again.

*Stop. Just stop.* She yanked her hand down and got back to work.

Before she'd pulled all the sugar peas and showed Owen how to decide which squash were ripe, she heard a car pull to a stop in front of the house. Not John-Parker's rumbling truck. Another tradesman perhaps?

The remodel was flying along, thanks to careful planning and John-Parker's diligent scheduling of construction workers. She kept a watchful eye on the budget the attorney had given them and he kept an eye on the workmen.

They were, she had to admit, a good team. Getting better all the time. The only thing they couldn't agree on was the most important.

She wondered where he'd gone this morning. An appointment, he'd claimed.

According to Taffy, who thought John-Parker was handsome with a capital *H*, people liked him. He went out of his way to be friendly and helpful.

But she'd also heard a handful of disparaging remarks and hateful comments. Zoey had heard them, too. Several people had even offered support of "her" side. Comments that pricked Zoey's conscience. John-Parker wasn't perfect, but he was not an outlaw.

A car door slammed.

Leaving the basket of fresh vegetables, but with the children in tow, she rounded the house, careful to avoid the discarded lumber that had yet to make its way into the giant dumpster. John-Parker's boys, as she'd come to think of Charlie and River, would take care of cleanup this afternoon.

Though she'd had serious doubts in the beginning, she'd come to agree with him about the teens. They worked hard, as if pleasing John-Parker—and her—meant something to them. She'd seen his hand on a shoulder, heard his quiet instructions, his strong but caring way of redirecting them when they got off track. They looked up to him. The way her son did.

Zoey turned the corner to see an unfamiliar white sedan parked along the side street in front of the house. A woman in a classy gray pantsuit got out, a folder in hand, and approached.

"Good morning. I'm Berkley Metcalfe from Children's Services. Is John-Parker Wisdom home?"

Zoey stiffened. This wasn't John-Parker's home. "He's not here at the moment. Is this about the boys?"

"In a manner of speaking. I'm here to start the home study he requested."

"Home study?" Zoey's heart jumped. What was John-Parker up to now? "What home study would that be?"

"For the residential home he plans to establish here. We have to make sure the home is suitable, start background checks, get forms signed, et cetera. A lot of paperwork."

"He can't do that. The town council hasn't yet approved his request."

The woman waved a hand. "He explained the situation to me on the phone, so this is a preliminary only, to get the ball rolling. Mr. Wisdom assures me the issue will be resolved, and since DCS is in desperate need for more foster homes for teenagers, we hope to expedite the process. Background checks can take weeks."

The woman droned on as if she were certain Zoey knew all about John-Parker's dealings. He'd gone behind her back. Again. Ordered a home study as if she had no say in the matter.

No wonder he'd been so sweet this morning. No wonder he'd kissed her on the forehead like a naïve child.

While she was struggling not to fall in love, he was setting her up for the kill.

By noon, John-Parker finished his errands and, feeling accomplished, picked up Chinese carry-out from the Golden Dragon and drove to Mamie's house. He was more of a Mexican cuisine guy, but Chinese occasionally was okay. Zoey and the kids liked Chinese. And they'd love the hand-dipped ice cream for dessert.

Three trucks were parked on the lawn outside the house. Roofers crawled on the shingles, their nail guns snapping. One great thing about small towns, the tradesmen were known to everyone and bad ones quickly disappeared. He had confidence in the handful of workers he'd hired to handle the complicated projects.

After a peck on the front door, he pushed it open and, in a teasing voice, called, "Honey, I'm ho-ome, and I bring noodles and egg rolls."

Zoey stormed into the living room, eyes blazing, mouth pressed into a tight line.

"You." She stalked toward him with a finger aimed like a spear to pierce his heart. "You went behind my back."

He blinked a couple of times. This was not the greeting he'd hoped for. "You've already heard about the council meeting?"

She jerked back, eyes widening. "What?"

"The town council meeting?" he asked slowly. "My talk with Mayor Jones this morning?"

Her head dropped back, eyes closed. A frustrated breath seeped from her lips like a fast-leaking tire. "More deceit. I should have known."

"I was going to tell you." Not that a rejection was anything to share, but her reaction was exactly what he did not want. "I only left the mayor half hour ago. How did you hear so quickly? And why aren't you ecstatic that he rejected my request?"

"We're not even on the same page, Mr. Wisdom. I'm talking about the social worker who showed up this morning to begin your home study."

His belly dropped. "Oh."

He was in so much trouble. He could see it in her eyes, hear it in her voice. She was ready to kick him to curb and never speak to him again.

This was not turning out to be his best day.

"I didn't know you had a meeting with the mayor. Now that I *do* know, I realize why you—" she sucked in a breath, her cheeks reddening. "—tried to manipulate me this morning."

"Manipulate?" Frowning, John-Parker rocked back on his heels. "How did I do that?"

"You know how." She turned her face to the side as if she couldn't bear to look at him. Her cheeks grew redder.

He sorted through his memory of this morning, trying to figure out where she was coming from. He'd played with the kids, fixed her coffee, talked about Mamie, and then he'd left.

*Oh*. He'd kissed her on the forehead.

"That was not manipulation, Zoey," he said quietly.

She whipped around to glare at him. "Then what was it?"

A very good but very disturbing question he'd asked himself several times.

"Well..." he said carefully. "I...care about you." A lot. "Don't you know that by now?"

She scoffed. But her lower lip trembled.

She'd better not cry. He was done for if she did. He could take a punch to the face, a kick in the shins, but he could not take tears from a lady. Especially this one. He'd fight a bear to keep her from crying.

"Hey. Hey." He moved closer and took hold of her shoulders.

She backed away. "Don't touch me. You claim to care, but you're sneaking around behind my back to take this house away from me and my kids. You're no different than any other jerk."

John-Parker's hands fell to his sides.

"No sneaking to it, Zoey. I meant to tell you about the home study." He raked a hand over his hair. "I wasn't expecting her this soon. We're not ready."

"We certainly are not, and we won't ever be. Even though she left a fat folder of papers to fill out." Zoey crossed her arms, expression stricken.

He knew body language. Used the skill extensively in his line of work, ever watchful for the bad actors.

Her body screamed hurt and rejection more than anger. But she was definitely angry. With him. Again.

"Zoey. You already knew my plans for this house. I've never given you any reason to believe that I've changed my mind. Those plans don't erase the feelings I have for you."

Even as John-Parker struggled with those feelings, he knew they couldn't go beyond this place and time. But that did not mean he'd intentionally cause her grief.

"I haven't changed mine either." Her eyes were glassy, her mouth trembling. If she'd heard his near declaration of love, she ignored it. She was hurt. He'd hurt her.

Everything in him wanted to offer comfort and convince her that she mattered.

Hands outstretched in a plea for understanding, he said, "Zoey. Hey, come on. Don't be upset. We can work this out."

She turned her back to him. "Go away, John-Parker. I can't talk to you right now. Just go."

He touched her shoulder. She flinched and, before he could say or do anything more to resolve the situation, she left him standing alone in the empty living room.

In ten seconds, he heard a door slam.

Heart heavy for reasons he was beginning to understand, John-Parker went down into the basement to speak to the contractors. Then, at loose ends and unwelcome inside the house that was half his, he drove back to his rental and made a video call to Brandt.

Zoey needed time to cool down. Time, he hoped, would get them back on even footing. He didn't want her to be angry or hurt. He wanted her to be…happy, safe, protected.

"I was about to call you." Not one for flowery greetings, Brandt's square-jawed face, honed physique and military haircut filled up the phone screen. "What's up in my least favorite town on the planet?"

John-Parker huffed a mirthless laugh. "Your timing is impeccable. As usual. For every step forward, I've taken two steps backward."

"Having issues with that old house?"

"Surprisingly few. The house is not the problem."

"The council?"

"Yeah." He shared the latest rejection. "Waiting until the end of July for another meeting leaves only a month to finish everything."

"Do everything you can up to that point."

"We are."

"We? As in Zoey. How are things in that corner?"

Had he talked to Brandt about Zoey? Probably. He'd told his business partner everything else about this visit to Rosemary Ridge that had not turned out anything like he'd expected. Zoey was a huge part of the unexpected.

"She ran me out of the house just now."

"Hmm. And you let her. Interesting that you didn't stand your ground as you normally would.

"Yeah." John-Parker pulled at his lower lip, saw the gesture in the corner thumbnail photo.

"You got feelings for this woman?"

John-Parker considered dumping the entire Zoey situation on his best friend. Was he ready to admit out loud that he could possibly, maybe, might, feel more than friendship for someone?

But as a couple, he and Zoey were impossible. Right? Friends, yes. Love, no. He had a life he loved, traveling all over the world, meeting interesting people. He had a business to run and an apartment he rarely saw back in Phoenix.

John-Parker could not allow himself to fall in love with anyone.

In the end, he simply admitted a different truth. "I don't want to take away her opportunity for a new start. I've even prayed about selling the house outright, the way she wants to."

"And?"

"It's wrong, Brandt. That big old house is meant to nurture teenagers, the way it did us. But Zoey matters, too."

Through the small video screen, Brandt squinted blue eyes at John-Parker. "So, you *are* falling for her."

"You know me better than that. Silent Security is my life. I have no place for family."

John-Parker glanced at his bedroom, a room like many others he'd rented in his travels. Functional. Efficient. No personal items. No photos. Not even of friends. Just like his apartment. Clean, organized and lonely.

Oddly, he hadn't made his bed this morning. Zoey had called. She'd needed him and he'd forgotten everything else in his rush to see her. "I like her. We work well together."

"When you're not fighting over the house?"

"Yeah. Strangely, we've agreed on most everything except that and a few tweaks on the remodel. The rec room idea you and I came up with? We're making an apartment down there for her and her kids. She can't afford to move out yet."

A temporary apartment. But if he didn't agree to sell, how would she afford to move later?

"You're getting in way too deep there, my man."

"You're right about that." The Zoey problem was giving him brain lock.

"What you need is some distance. How about taking a weekend assignment in California?"

Work. He loved protecting people. He missed it. Concentrating on staying alive and keeping a paying client hale and hearty would require his full concentration. The best kind of distraction from a particular dark-eyed woman.

"Tell me about this gig."

Brandt laid out what amounted to an easy weekend of work. Fly out tonight. Subtly protect a certain paranoia-prone celebrity. Fly back Sunday.

Brandt was right. The distance from Zoey and the overwhelming responsibility of Mamie's will would clear his head. Maybe even clear his heart.

"I'm in. Send me the details."

After a quick call to Lonnie Buckner to make sure a weekend away was permitted, he packed his bags, called the airline and headed to the Tulsa airport.

He considered texting Zoey but refrained. She'd kicked him out. The ball was in her court. She probably wouldn't care that he was gone as long as his absence didn't affect her inheritance. She wouldn't miss him.

He hoped he could say the same about her.

River and Charlie arrived after school as usual, but John-Parker didn't return. The boys had not heard from him, either, but that wasn't unusual.

After Zoey fed them a peanut butter and jelly sandwich and milk, their usual snack, both teens got to work cleaning up the construction rubble left in the backyard.

Owen begged to stay with the big boys, but she refused, citing the dangers of nails and who knew what. Uncharacteristically, her son sulked and asked for John-Parker.

And that frustrated her.

Twice she took out her phone to text the man. Twice she shoved the device back into her pocket.

She was still angry over what she considered his deception, no matter that he claimed innocence.

For the second time now, he'd gone behind her back. She couldn't let herself trust him.

Except, of late, she had. Like her son, she missed him when

he wasn't there. Even when he was working downstairs in the basement and she was on the main floor sorting through the boxes and cabinets and closets, she listened for his voice, especially his laugh.

He'd come up out of the basement wearing construction dust and a tired grin, asking for some of her famous sweet tea, and she'd be swamped with feelings she shouldn't have. Happy feelings.

Her traitorous heart had started to want more than friendship from John-Parker Wisdom. They'd shared so much together in these past weeks and had become close.

Or so she'd thought. Until his latest underhanded play.

She was a slow learner when it came to relationships.

Frustrated and perplexed, she toted the suitcase filled with Mamie's mysterious life down the stairs and began to sort documents by date and type, reading as she went. Anything to get her mind off John-Parker.

After the children napped and she hadn't, she loaded them into their car seats and headed for the nursing home. The elders seemed to enjoy the company of her little ones and the interaction would take her mind off John-Parker.

It didn't.

Why hadn't John-Parker called or texted? Where was he? They had work to do. Owen was asking.

Maybe she'd overreacted. She should have given him the benefit of the doubt.

Gnawing her fingernails, she stewed and fretted, all the while trying to put on a happy face for the elderly residents of Brookhaven.

Finally, while Owen and Olivia colored with two grandmotherly residents, Zoey relented and shot a text to John-Parker.

Silence. No reply. Nothing.

He still hadn't replied by the time they'd left Brookhaven.

John-Parker must be furious. Shutting her out. Abandoning her.

Back home—her home for now, anyway—River and Charlie wandered in and out to ask about John-Parker. At dinnertime, her appetite gone, Zoey fed them the rewarmed Chinese, noting that the longer John-Parker stayed away, the more solemn and gloomy River became. He didn't say a word during the meal.

Maybe she should text John-Parker again for River's sake.

John-Parker's desire to teach these boys a better way pushed in. Hygiene, job skills, manners and good character were important things every kid needed. Weren't those the things she was teaching Owen?

But who was watching out for a moody, glowering kid with a bad attitude, like River?

John-Parker wanted to. So did she. She sympathized with the boy, even as his attitude aggravated her. John-Parker saw through his shell to the wounded child. The more she looked at things through John-Parker's eyes, the more she questioned herself and her goals.

All kids needed guidance. All kids mattered.

Unlike the teenagers John-Parker wanted to help, Owen and Olivia had a healthy, loving parent in their lives.

Could she make a living for her children if she forfeited her half of Mamie's house for the sake of kids who had no one else? As Owen and Olivia's only parent, her responsibility was to her own children, not someone else's. Wasn't it?

*Oh, Mamie, I wish you were here to guide me. I wish God would listen to me the way you said He does.*

The dilemma ate at her.

"I'm out of here." River shoved back from the table. To Charlie, he said, "You coming?"

"Owen wants to play Legos." Charlie's round face was hopeful. Inside, he was still a child.

For a nanosecond, River's expression softened. "Suit yourself."

Then he spun on his dirty tennis shoes and slouched out of the house.

With worried eyes, Charlie watched the other boy leave. "I wish John-Parker was here."

Zoey took out her phone to text John-Parker yet again, but changed her mind and put the device back in her pocket. She was not going to chase the man.

He'd gone behind her back. She couldn't get past that. He was probably out there right now finding a way to cheat her out of this property.

Part of her believed he'd do such a thing. Most of her didn't.

John-Parker confused her. His actions confused her. His sudden absence confused her. Even though she'd sent him away, Zoey had expected him to return and remind her that this was his property, too.

She didn't hear from him that day or the next. Saturday morning, the social worker brought River and Charlie to the house again.

They were disappointed to learn John-Parker had not checked in.

River kicked a porch step. The kid hadn't washed his hair and it flopped like oily black strings onto his cheeks. "Where is he?"

"I'm not sure. I texted him but he didn't answer." One text. And a long restless night of wondering where he was, why he hadn't replied, and if she'd ever see him again.

"Text him again," Charlie insisted. "He might have been in a dead zone."

True. She hadn't thought of that. Hilly areas around Rosemary Ridge and long stretches of rural highway were notoriously devoid of cell service.

Removing the device from her skirt pocket, she opened the texting app and stared at his name and phone number.

"I don't know what to say."

"Tell him he's a liar." River, whose mood was worse than last night, glared at her and then stomped toward the backyard.

Charlie blinked startled eyes and then shot Zoey one unhappy glance before following his troubled buddy.

Zoey stared morosely after the boys.

Hadn't she called John-Parker a liar herself? After hearing the words from someone else, she knew they were not true. John-Parker had never lied. Just because he didn't share his minute-by-minute agenda did not constitute lying.

Zoey stared at her cell phone for long seconds, uncertain of what to do.

She didn't want to send a gushy text that sounded needy or lonely or, even worse, besotted. Nor did she want him to think he'd won by giving her the silent treatment.

Finally, she typed in a quick message.

Call me.

In seconds the reply came.

Working. Can't talk. Later.

Working? He'd gone back to Phoenix or to where ever a personal bodyguard worked?

Zoey's body tensed, but not with anger. With a sudden, unexpected adrenaline-charged fear. John-Parker's job meant putting himself between danger and a client, even if that danger was a bullet.

Her fertile mind imagined all kinds of frightening scenarios.

Where was he? What if something happened to him?

He infuriated her at times, but she never wanted anything bad to happen to him. She wanted him safe, here with the boys…and her.

A phrase she'd read in Mamie's Bible came to her. A verse she'd found peculiarly comforting. Maybe not the exact wording, but the meaning. Something about not being afraid because Jesus is always with us. She wanted to believe, as Mamie and John-Parker did, that Someone all-powerful and loving was ever-present and watching over her and the people she loved.

Zoey closed her eyes and, for the second time in recent days, whispered a prayer.

*If You're real and You hear me, please be with John-Parker and keep him safe. I don't want to lose him.*

Except, he wasn't hers to lose.

John-Parker was exhausted. He rotated a sore shoulder.

Twenty-four-plus hours of babysitting Mo Rich, a reckless celebrity, who spent half his time snorting cocaine and the other half endangering himself with outrageous behavior while crazed fans shrieked and tried to break into his car, his performance venue, and his hotel room.

"Charge him double, even triple, next time," John-Parker told Brandt as he waited to board his return flight to Tulsa. "Give me a Guatemala guerrilla any day over spoiled, erratic entertainers."

He'd handled plenty of ruckuses over popular celebrities, but he was accustomed to controlling the crowds without injury to anyone. Usually, the client cooperated. Mo Rich the rapper, worked his fans to a frenzy and then invited them to party with him. They'd gone nuts.

John-Parker's shoulder was bruised from being gang-tackled into a car door while shoving Mo to safety inside.

He hadn't expected anything as crazed. Was he losing his edge? Had he not planned for every variable the way he usually did? His line of work required absolute focus.

Was Mamie's house and Zoey becoming a distraction he couldn't afford?

While he fretted, keeping his concerns to himself, Brandt agreed to make a note on the man's record and hung up. John-Parker boarded his flight, his thoughts going back to Zoey and the kids.

He'd missed them. Even though cocaine-head had kept him on his toes, thoughts of Zoey had kept crowding in.

She was a problem he must resolve.

He opened his phone to shoot her a quick text and then remembered. She was mad at him. She was probably even madder by now. A text wasn't long enough to sort out their disagreements.

Face to face was the best way of resolving issues.

He'd be home in a few hours. They'd talk then.

Man, he'd missed her, missed the kids, the noise and excitement of the remodel. If he hadn't been so busy with a gangster-turned-rapper, he'd have tried a video call.

She'd probably have hung up on him.

With a sigh, he settled back for the flight, eyes closed, eager to be home.

His eyes popped open.

Home?

When had he started thinking of Rosemary Ridge as home?

# Chapter Thirteen

"It's about time you showed up. Are you okay?

Zoey's heart ricocheted off her rib cage. John-Parker was back. Standing on the front porch, obviously exhausted, but in one piece.

Thank God. And she really meant that. God must have heard her prayer because John-Parker had returned. And he looked like every dream she'd had for the last two nights.

After all her inner arguments against him, she had to grip the doorframe to keep from jumping into his arms.

"Didn't think you cared." His tone was cool, his expression watchful, as if he expected a battle.

Not tonight. She was too relieved to see him. Too…grateful to have him back. Taffy, with her nose for news and celebrities had dropped by with a social media video that scared Zoey silly. John-Parker had been in LA protecting one of the most law-breaking rappers in the business. A former, possibly current, gang member with a rap sheet a mile long.

"I saw what happened. That mob. You could have been killed."

"No big deal. I'm fine." He blew off her concern as if he'd been on a vacation for a week. "Let's talk about something else."

Was this what he did for a living on a regular basis? When he'd told her about his security work, she'd envisioned the guys at high-end retailers with earpieces, black suits and suspicious stares, not criminals.

"You should have told me where you were headed."

"As I recall, you were furious when I left here. You actually kicked me out of my own house."

Her lips curved. "Half a house."

"Right." The impish grin she'd come to adore appeared.

"The boys wondered where you were." She pushed the storm door open. Welcoming him, blood singing and pulse dancing to have him home again.

John-Parker's long legs brought him into the house. "What about you? Did you miss me? I missed you."

If he hadn't added the last three words, she'd have remained strong. But here he was, standing so close and all in one piece that she could feel him breathe.

"Maybe a little," she admitted.

Somehow her hand had hold of his upper arm. He looked down at it and then found her eyes with his. The storm clouds gathered in the gray depths—a completely different kind of storm. One that rumbled inside her as well, a storm of confusion and attraction.

Was he as bewildered by her as she was by him?

Before she had time to reconsider, she moved in for a casual hello hug. At least, that's what she told herself.

As her arms bracketed his, John-Parker flinched.

Zoey stepped back. "Are you hurt?"

"It's nothing this won't fix." He reached for her. "Come back here."

Kicking the door behind him closed with one foot, he circled her waist and waltzed her backward into the empty living room.

She knew he was going to kiss her. She also knew he would tell her nothing about his injury until he was ready.

She put two fingers against his lips. "Is this wise?"

"Necessary," he murmured. "Healing."

Then his mouth found hers.

Had she lost her mind? What was she doing?

As quickly as those inner protests came, they disappeared in the sweetest, most tender kiss of her life. His lips asked and she answered, seeking she knew not what, but finding a beauty she thirsted for.

Zoey had had plenty of kisses, but this was different. Just as John-Parker was different.

Hadn't they been leading up to this moment for weeks? Curious about the buzz of energy between them, even when they argued? She couldn't stay mad at John-Parker, and the truth was, she didn't want to.

And now, in this breathless moment of pleasure and longing, Zoey felt treasured, protected.

Yet John-Parker was supposed to be her competitor.

He *was* her competitor. Wasn't he?

The awful imp that plagued her with insecurities started yammering in her ear. Was John-Parker pretending to care so she'd give up her half of the house?

Untangling arms that had somehow found their way around John-Parker's neck, Zoey stepped away from what was the best kiss of her life. A kiss she would never forget. One that went beyond desire to love.

As much as she wanted to believe in love, she was afraid of the consequences.

She touched her mouth, felt the hammering of her pulse in her ears. "Why did you do that?"

Why had she?

John-Parker's mouth—oh, that wonderfully expressive mouth—tilted. "You can't stand in the doorway looking that beautiful and expect a man not to want to kiss you."

She pressed a palm to each burning cheek. "Don't be nice. I know why you kissed me."

"If you're thinking anything other than what just happened, you're wrong. I missed you. I'm glad to be back. I'm sorry we quarreled."

She watched his face for any hint of subterfuge. All she saw was sincerity. And that further disoriented her suspicious, cynical mind. Men lied. They were seldom honest unless it suited their agenda. Then they died and left her alone.

John-Parker could die. He could have died this weekend.

"What happened in LA?"

If her change of subjects surprised him, John-Parker didn't let on.

She sure didn't want to talk about or think about kissing him. If she did, she'd be tempted to walk right back into his arms and kiss him at least a dozen times.

She had to be smarter than that. Especially now that she knew more about his occupation.

Oh, what a tangle this was. Why had Mamie done this to them?

John-Parker carefully, slowly slid off his suit jacket and layered it over the back of the only chair in the room.

"Let me grab a sandwich and then we'll talk." He leaned in for a quick disconcerting peck on the lips before heading for the kitchen.

Okay, she could kiss him without going bonkers. Kisses were nice.

Following him into the kitchen, she took sliced ham and cheese from the fridge. "The apartment is almost complete."

"That was fast." John-Parker pulled bread and a paper towel from the pantry and settled at the scarred table. "Did the contractor estimate when you could move in?"

"Soon, but that's not important. Tell me about your injury. Did you see a doctor?"

"Zoey, I'm fine. A bruise, okay? I bumped the sharp edge of a car door. Don't make a big deal of it."

"I saw what happened, John-Parker."

He put his sandwich together without looking at her. "Yeah?"

"Big stars like Mo Rich can't move a muscle without someone posting on social media. Usually him." She pulled out her phone and opened the app. "Look."

She stuck the phone in front of his face.

John-Parker bit into his ham and cheese as he watched. He shrugged, but only with one shoulder, the uninjured side. "Looks worse than it was."

She doubted that.

"Do you get into situations like this all the time?"

"Not often. I'm usually better at my job. Got any chips?"

"Don't change the subject."

"No use wasting breath about a bruise. Tell me what's been going on since I left. How are the kids? The boys? Any more interesting discoveries in that suitcase?"

Zoey slapped a hand to her mouth. "Oh, my goodness, yes." In her concern for John-Parker's injury and her thrill at having him home—and kissing her—she'd temporarily forgotten. "I found something of yours."

John-Parker paused, the sandwich halfway to his mouth. "Something of mine? What? Did you find my Peyton Manning rookie card?"

She wished her find was that simple. Hopefully, this wouldn't come as a shock.

She fluttered the back of a hand in his direction and said, "Eat. I'll be right back."

Leaving the kitchen, she went into Mamie's quarters, now empty of everything except the suitcase contents she'd spread on the floor in sorted piles.

She'd pondered the documents in the old suitcase since discovering them last night after the babies were asleep. The information bothered her. John-Parker had never once mentioned it, even when they'd shared stories from their childhoods.

She knew about his parents' untimely deaths when he was eleven, but did he know this? Was he simply too private to tell her?

Either way, how would he react once he knew that she knew?

As she returned to the kitchen, Zoey pressed the oversize manila envelope tightly against her thudding heart. John-Parker sat at the end of the table, a half-emptied glass of milk and a bag of potato chips at his elbow, a nearly eaten sandwich in one hand.

"You *were* hungry." She slid the envelope in front of him. "I hope I haven't pried into your personal life too much. I didn't mean to. Don't be mad at me."

He glanced at her and then at the envelope, his forehead

wrinkled in a frown. "That sounds ominous. I guess you didn't find my Peyton Manning card, huh? I wish I could find it. My dad gave it to me."

His dad. Zoey blanched at the single word.

"Sorry. No. Have you seen these documents? Did you know about them?"

"Now, I'm really curious. What's in there?" He put the sandwich aside, wiped his hands and opened the flap. "Is this a good find or a bad one?"

"You be the judge of that." What if he hadn't been told? What if the contents of that envelope came as a shock? What if he resented the fact that she'd pried into his personal business?

He slid the stack of papers out, pushed the envelope aside and began to read the legal paperwork.

Biting the edge of her thumbnail, Zoey watched his expression and knew the moment he realized what he held in his hands.

His mouth dropped open. He blinked. Read again. Flipped page after page before he dropped the papers to the tabletop and leaned back against the chair.

For the longest moments, while the house creaked from the brisk Oklahoma wind, he said nothing. She waited, not wanting to rush him with questions.

He closed his eyes. A scowl tugged at his scarred eyebrow. She understood then. He hadn't known.

Wow. Just wow.

Finally, he opened his eyes and spoke, his voice quiet and stunned.

"I was adopted?"

John-Parker's insides tumbled and sloshed. His mind rolled with questions. He couldn't have been more shocked if Zoey had hit him in the face with a flaming log.

Her voice brought him into focus. "You didn't know."

He shook his head. "No idea. Until this moment, I was the only child of John and Erica Wisdom, named John for my dad and Parker for my mom's maiden name. When I was small, I begged them for a sibling. It never occurred to me that they couldn't have more. I never questioned and they never mentioned that I was anything other than their biological son."

"Does it bother you to know?"

He pondered for a beat before shaking his head. Right now, he wasn't sure of anything except the shock. "I'm surprised and wonder why they never told me, but they were great parents. Until their accident, I had a happy childhood."

"Maybe they were waiting until you were older to tell you."

"Maybe." The old familiar wound he rarely visited opened inside his chest. Mom and Dad were gone. He would never know if they'd intended to tell him or why they hadn't.

"Why did Mamie have your paperwork? Why didn't *she* ever tell you?"

"Good questions." He tapped a finger on the legal papers. "But this document explains one thing."

"What's that?"

"Why none of my extended family stepped up to take me after Mom and Dad died. Dad was an only child, like me. His dad was deceased and his mother in a memory-care facility. But my mom had a brother, even though we only saw him and his wife at Christmas. After Mom was killed, I never saw them again. Now, I know why."

"You think they didn't take you because they knew you weren't biologically related?"

The ham and cheese lay heavy on his belly. "Looks that way, doesn't it?"

"Wow." Zoey puffed out her cheeks and released a gusty exhale. "I thought my family history was ugly. That's cold."

The rejection still hurt but not as much as it once had. He'd become an orphan long ago. Twice. Once at birth and then at age eleven, though he'd only discovered those facts tonight. His parents—the adoptive ones—had loved him. But he couldn't help wondering about the others; the first parents who'd given him away.

John-Parker rubbed a hand down his shirtfront. The bruised shoulder tweaked much worse than the wound in his heart.

He was a man now. Though he'd grieved his adoptive parents for a long time, and never known his birth family, the past was behind him. All of it. Mamie had been the surrogate parent he'd needed.

He had healed. Mostly. If the rejection resurfaced at times like this, he supposed that was normal. And if he was curious about his birth parents, that was normal, too.

His past was as much of a mystery as Mamie's.

The words of Calpernia, the homeless woman, suddenly came back to him. She'd rambled about his purpose in Rosemary Ridge and something about a mystery. *His* mystery. Was this what she'd meant? But how could she know anything about him, a total stranger?

A tingle started at the back of his neck. The kind that only happened on the job when a situation was not quite the way it seemed. The tingle he'd experienced Saturday night right before a rabid fan had slammed into his back while another had shoved him against the car door and kidney-punched him.

Mamie, supposedly a stranger, had taken him, an eleven-year-old boy, into her home filled with teenagers. He'd been the only preteen she'd ever raised.

Zoey must have noticed his pensive mood. She rubbed her hand up and down his forearm in a soothing, comforting motion, the way he'd seen her soothe Olivia and Owen when they had a boo-boo.

Now she stroked his arm as if her touch could shield him from the wounds of his past.

Maybe she could.

Her kiss had sure faded the memory of his lousy weekend.

"What are you thinking?" she asked. "You have a funny look on your face. Are you okay?"

"Lots of thoughts racing through my head right now." Mamie. The adoption. Zoey. Most of all, her.

"I'm sorry. Should I have kept this from you?"

The tender compassion in her voice brought a lump to his throat. He cleared his throat, but the emotion remained.

"No. Absolutely not. Being adopted answers some questions I've had."

"But opens up others, right?"

He nodded. "Like, why did Mamie have my adoption papers? Why didn't I know they existed? Why did she agree to foster an eleven-year-old when teenagers were her calling? And does any of this have something to do with the reason she made me an heir?"

*And when can I kiss you again?*

"Maybe there was a connection between the two of you before you came into her care." Suddenly, her mouth dropped open. She pressed a nail-bitten hand to her chest. "John-Parker, could she have been your birth mother? And when she learned of your adoptive parents' deaths, she asked for you?"

The notion rocked him back in his chair. He blinked. Mamie? His biological mother?

After the initial shock, he rejected the idea. "Couldn't be. She had a husband and two sons. Why would she have given a third child up for adoption?"

Zoey nodded decisively. "You're right. Mamie loved kids too much. She certainly wouldn't have given up a bio child. There must be a connection here, though. Too many pieces of this puzzle don't fit."

John-Parker agreed, and he would keep digging until he knew more. For now, processing the shocking news that he'd been adopted was enough to keep him occupied.

Well, that and kissing Zoey.

His cell phone chimed. Glad for the interruption to a barrage of baffling thoughts, he answered the call.

Three minutes later, he was out the door.

River was in trouble.

Sunday evening should have been a quiet time of relaxation. Instead, every five minutes, Zoey glanced at her cell phone to be sure she hadn't missed a text or call from John-Parker concerning River. She alternately checked on her sleeping children and sorted through more boxes from the attic. Much was useless junk, relegated to a black garbage bag.

She was still coming to grips with John-Parker's adoption shock, but even more with the growing relationship between the two of them.

No one had ever made her feel as precious and important as she'd felt when he held her close.

"This can't happen," she said to the empty room and wondered if God was listening the way John-Parker claimed. "His job scares me. We're from different places. He's supposed to be my competitor."

She latched onto the latter, aware that her fear of losing the house had mysteriously faded into the background. Not completely, but enough that she was more concerned about John-Parker getting hurt in his dangerous line of work than about the money from the sale of this house.

Letting her heart get involved had done that.

When would she learn? Kisses didn't mean anything to a guy but a good time.

Hadn't John-Parker's silence this weekend been reason enough to suspect that his intentions were mere fun and games? When their time was up, he'd be out the door with a kiss and a wave but no regrets.

But did she really believe that about him?

With a groan, she dropped a stack of moth-eaten linens into a garbage bag and intentionally refocused her conflicted thoughts away from John-Parker and on to River.

What had happened? According to the tiny bit of information John-Parker had shot at her as he'd jogged to his truck, the police had arrested the boy and he refused to talk to anyone expect John-Parker.

If the babies hadn't already been in bed for the night, she'd have gone with him.

Or not.

Yes, she would have. And there she went again, flip-flopping back and forth more than a politician.

This weekend should have been enough to prove how unimportant she was to him. He'd left without a word, without so much as a call, leaving her to worry that he would forfeit their inheritance. And her.

But now he was back, kissing her as if he'd missed her as much as she'd missed him.

She pressed a hand to each side of her face, her insides in a rampage. Her emotions and thoughts had never been quite so topsy-turvy.

John-Parker Wisdom with his easy ways made her wish for things she shouldn't. Wanting a man to love her had been her downfall before, but in spite of past experience, she'd begun wishing John-Parker would remain in Rosemary Ridge and in her life forever.

Not that she would let him know. He belonged in Phoenix and couldn't wait to get back to work full-time. Work that frightened her.

The last thing she needed was a man who lived life in the danger zone. Being widowed once was more than enough. If she let herself love him, something bad would happen, something that left her alone and hurting.

Everyone else in her life had left her. Her parents. The grandma who'd raised her. Her husband. Even Aunt Mamie. John-Parker had already promised to leave. Why couldn't she get the message? No one stayed.

*Jesus will never leave you.*

The thought came out of nowhere. Or, more likely, out of a stressed-out mind.

She dragged two filled garbage bags of discards to the garage. Someone had opened a box and scattered its contents on the garage floor. With a sigh, she reorganized the items, and then stepped outside the garage light and into the dark summer night, careful not to trip over any construction odds and ends.

The inky sky was clear and speckled with brilliant twinkling stars.

The day's revelations rolled through her mind. Kisses. John-Parker's injury. His adoption documents. The why questions neither of them could answer. Now, River was in trouble.

She felt sorry for John-Parker. Although he maintained a calm acceptance of the adoption situation, he must be shaken. Yet he'd left his own shocking situation to focus on the teenager he tried so hard to mentor.

What would happen to the boys after he left?

"Hey, pretty lady." A deep voice came out of the darkness.

Zoey jumped…and squealed. Adrenaline spurted into veins even as her brain registered the familiar voice.

John-Parker appeared out of the shadows.

"You!" Zoey bopped him on his good arm. "You scared me."

With a laugh, he pulled her close. "Sorry. Not sorry."

"Ha, ha. You are so not funny."

"Yes, I am." He stared down at her mouth. "You're laughing."

"Am not."

But she was.

His lips curved, teasing. "No fear, m'lady, I'm an expert. I'll protect you."

"Will you?" The question was half joke, half pathetic plea.

The teasing left John-Parker's face. "With my life."

At his serious tone, she stilled, wishing she could believe that she mattered that much. But John-Parker protected people for money, not because he loved them. Yet the tender tone in his voice and the way he held her, lightly, securely, stirred the yearning in her again.

Hope and bad experience tumbled over each other like golf balls in a clothes dryer.

"Would you really?" she finally asked.

"Don't you know by now? You mean a lot to me. Didn't expect it to happen, but there it is."

He kept his words easy and casual but sincere.

"I care about you, too, John-Parker, but—"

He pressed his fingers to her lips. "No buts. Let's look at the stars together and talk about anything except those pesky buts. You can't see stars like this in the city."

"Do you miss it? Phoenix?" The reminder of where he belonged would help keep her head on straight.

"Not as much as I expected to."

A relative non-answer. Which meant she shouldn't press him on the topic, no matter how much she wanted to.

Expect nothing, but enjoy the good things that came along. Hadn't she tried to live by that slogan? Like now, when John-Parker's strong bodyguard arms held her as if she was special. She wasn't. Not really. He was a natural guardian who'd protect anyone, not only her and the children.

The reminder was enough to keep her emotions in check.

"How's River?" Safe ground. And she wanted to know.

"He's okay now." John-Parker shifted them around so that her back was against him, his muscled arm cradling her waist. He rested his chin lightly on her hair and exhaled a weary sigh. "He was caught tagging the underpass on the edge of town."

"Tagging? As in painting graffiti?"

"Mmm-hmm. The county sheriff didn't take kindly to his idea of artistic expression."

"I've seen his drawings. He's very talented."

"If he would only channel that talent in the right direction instead of painting angry images on other people's property."

"He was very upset while you were gone, John-Parker. Gloomy, surly, angry."

"I know. Believe me, he blasted me good. He thought I'd ghosted him, his belligerent term for abandonment."

Against her back, Zoey felt the rise and fall of John-Parker's chest, the beat of his heart. He was anxious for the boy, as well as exhausted from his weekend, but she couldn't make herself move away.

"He knows you're only here temporarily, John-Parker, and that you have no intention of staying." She didn't want the admission to hurt, but it did. "You haven't lied to him." Nor to her. John-Parker *cared* for all of them, but he was still leaving as soon as the conditions of the will were met.

And the clock ticked louder every day.

"Yeah." He sighed again.

She wondered what that single word and soft sigh meant but didn't ask. Even though she knew he'd leave once the house was finished, she didn't want confirmation. Not tonight.

The summer night was warm and beautiful, and standing under the stars with a handsome man pleased the romantic girl she'd thought had died long ago. Only for this night, she let herself enjoy the girlish dream.

A summer romance, she thought, and grabbed hold of the concept. People had summer romances all the time. They knew the score from the beginning. Enjoy the summer. Then, come September, they'd part with no regrets and take with them only good memories.

Tonight, she was content and happy with John-Parker's warm breath against her hair, his muscled arms holding her secure. That was enough. It had to be.

She pressed her cheek against his shoulder in a kind of hug and John-Parker responded with a kiss to her ear.

Zoey smiled. Ear and forehead kissing had taken on a new meaning.

They talked a while, moving from concerns about River to John-Parker's weekend, her online job, her excitement over the basement apartment, and a dozen other topics until the Milky Way streaked white and beautiful above.

When John-Parker yawned for the third time, she said, "You should go home."

"Home," he said, and Zoey wondered at the wistful tone.

"I'd love to be out here with you until the sun rises," she

said, giving him another cheek hug, "but you've had a full weekend."

"Would you?" Again she heard the wistful flavor in his voice.

Her pulse skipped a couple of beats. "Yes."

He rocked her back and forth, their bodies in a stationary waltz beneath the stars. "This is good. Being here with you. Looking at the stars. Decompressing. Peaceful."

"Peaceful? How is that possible with all that's going on?"

"This may sound weird to you, but when I look at the stars, I feel God's presence. He brings me the kind of peace I can't get anywhere else."

"About that."

He stopped swaying and dipped around to look at her. "About what? Peace? God?"

"I'm reading Mamie's Bible, and the strangest thing keeps happening."

"Like what? You feel God's presence?"

"No, not exactly. But the words seem to come up off the pages as if they're meant for me to notice."

"They'll do that. Because they are."

"But how? The Bible is just an old book. Real old."

"The Bible may be ancient, but the message never stops being relevant. If your heart is open, God speaks to you through the verses."

"Now, *that* is weird."

He chuckled. "Want me to preach you another sermon?"

Zoey smiled up at the stars. God's stars. Hers and John-Parker's. If only for tonight.

As long as she could hear John-Parker's voice and feel him close, he could preach all he wanted.

# *Chapter Fourteen*

John-Parker was getting antsy.

Time raced past like a greyhound and though he went right on creating the kind of home and property that would nurture teenage boys, he knew he had a less than fifty-fifty chance of ever seeing that dream become reality. The council had spoken once. Then the mayor had refused his request for a special meeting. Now, he was in hurry-up-and-wait mode for the last meeting before time ran out, knotted up inside that he'd have to disappoint River and Charlie…and Mamie. Most of all, Mamie.

How could he leave knowing he'd failed her all over again? Knowing he'd never absolve the guilt and regret or find forgiveness? Aware that she was disappointed in him?

Added to his agenda was the nagging reality that he'd been adopted. Somewhere out in the world, he could have living relatives. Had they been aware of his birth mother's pregnancy? Of his existence? If they knew, did they care? Where was his mother? What happened to her and his father?

Someone had to know the truth. Just as someone had to know if his adoption was in any way connected to Mamie.

He'd wrestled a dozen scenarios, and a connection outside of routine foster care was the only one that made sense.

But what was that connection?

He'd made an appointment to discuss the situation with Lonnie Buckner in case the attorney knew any more about him. Buckner and Mamie had apparently been close. He handled her estate, her will, and kept a watch on the budget for the remodel. John-Parker was convinced the man knew more than he'd told. He had to know why Mamie had left money to someone she hadn't seen in fifteen years.

The whys kept him awake at night.

Carrying all this in his head, John-Parker jogged down the newly finished basement stairs. "Ready to go?"

An excited Zoey stood in what was now an open-concept living and kitchen area divided by a white quartz island. "I love how this turned out."

The apartment only lacked paint and furnishings to be move-in ready. He liked the way the space looked, too. Zoey could live here for now, but the possibilities for future uses were endless. The compromise had been a win for both of them.

"I was thinking the same."

For the next few weeks, this would be her home. Beyond that, he'd already decided to help her find another place and pay for it if she'd let him. Only until she got on her feet. He didn't like the idea of her or the kids doing without.

His smartwatch flashed a notification.

"We'd better go. Our appointment's in fifteen minutes."

She made a face. "You and your obsessive punctuality."

"Blame Miss Mamie. According to her rules, if you weren't at least ten minutes early, you were late. Punctuality, she'd say, is respect for other people. Being late is selfishness."

Zoey's smile widened. "You sound like her. Let me kiss the kids and remind Taffy where we're headed, and I'll meet you out front." She spun in a circle one last time. "You have good ideas, Mr. W."

He winked. "Keep thinking that way."

She made another face and jogged up the steps.

Cute. Real cute.

He followed her up, the manila envelope holding his mysterious past in hand, and headed out the door to his truck.

By the time they reached Buckner and Buckner Law Offices, nervous butterflies had taken up residence in his belly.

He was rarely anxious.

He wiped damp hands down his pant leg. Zoey noticed. "Nervous?"

"Some." The truth was he was more nervous than the first

time he'd faced the business end of a .380 semiautomatic. He was trained to handle physical threats. Emotional ones were a whole different ballgame.

Zoey picked up the manila envelope he'd put on the console between them. "We got this."

She leaned close to pat his shoulder but stopped. He'd healed quickly, as usual, but Zoey still pestered him about the injury.

He kind of liked the attention.

Inside the law offices, the receptionist recognized them from their scheduled visits. "How's the house coming along?"

In no mood for idle chatter, John-Parker was glad when Zoey replied.

With his mind on the adoption situation, he soon lost track of their conversation.

The inner-office door opened and Lonnie Buckner appeared. "Come on in."

The butterflies swarmed up into his chest. Zoey squeezed the top of his hand and followed him into the office.

She'd offered to come along if he'd wanted her to. Although accustomed to handling life on his own, he'd jumped at the offer. Having Zoey at his side felt right. She'd been the one to discover the adoption paperwork. They were in this thing together.

"I see you two are no longer at each other's throats. Congratulations."

John-Parker's grin was sheepish. "We're working things out."

More than getting along these days, they were…whatever they were.

"Good to know." With a dignified nod, the attorney took a seat behind his desk. "So, what are these questions you have for me today?"

John-Parker handed over the folder containing his adoption papers. "Can you tell me anything more about this?"

After a questioning glance at John-Parker, Buckner slipped on a pair of readers, withdrew the documents and flipped through them.

Slowly he removed the glasses and looked up. "What are your questions? Specifically."

"Were you aware that I was adopted?"

"Mamie shared that information with me, yes."

"Why didn't she tell me?"

Buckner glanced at the papers again and folded his hands atop them. A slight frown creased the space between his graying eyebrows.

He obviously had answers.

John-Parker leaned forward, fingers tight against his upper thighs. He knew his intensity showed and wanted it to. This was his life. He had a right, a need, to learn what he could.

"I want to know everything you do. All of it."

"The story is complicated, John-Parker, but Mamie left the information in my care for a reason. She thought someday you might have questions."

"She left these papers for me to find, didn't she?"

"Mamie hoped for your return, yes, and hoped to have the opportunity to answer these questions herself."

The statement was an indictment.

John-Parker hadn't returned in time. Another failure. Another way he'd disappointed Miss Mamie.

Guilt was a sharp knife slicing him into pieces he had no way of recovering.

He swallowed the dismay and did his best to focus on the here and now. The past was done. He could not change it. But, oh, how he wished he could.

"This is my story, Mr. Buckner. Mamie planned to tell me at some point, so I'd appreciate hearing it now from you."

"All right. As I said, your past is complicated and certain unknowns remain that could be…difficult. When you were a teenager, Mamie thought you were too young and unstable to know everything."

"Including why she fostered an eleven-year-old?"

The attorney's mouth curved but his eyes remained serious. "The story doesn't begin there, John-Parker."

"We know her husband and sons died in a car crash before she moved to Rosemary Ridge."

"You've been researching."

"We have, but information on adoptees is more difficult to find than car accidents and death certificates. My birth certificate lists John and Erica Wisdom as my parents. But they're also listed on the adoption papers. So, what's the story?"

Buckner rose and went to a small refrigerator. "Would you like some water? This could take a while."

"I'd appreciate a bottle. Thank you." His mouth was dry as the Mojave. "Zoey?"

"Yes, thank you."

What John-Parker wanted most was knowledge, but he took the offered bottle and unscrewed the cap while waiting for Buckner to retake his seat.

The attorney took a long drink then recapped the container before beginning.

"Mamie had a sister."

John-Parker sat up straight. Shock ricocheted down his back. "She did?"

He glanced at Zoey whose mouth fell open, her eyes widening. How many surprises were they in for?

"According to Mamie," Mr. Buckner went on, "Charlese was as different from her as any sister could be. Here are where the unknowns begin. Mamie knew Charlese became pregnant and gave the child up for adoption. She didn't know the father, and Charlese wouldn't say. Mamie also knew the child was a boy."

Zoey sucked in a breath.

John-Parker's pulse kicked into high gear. "Am I that child? Was Mamie my aunt? Was that why she included me in her will?"

Buckner held up a hand. "We don't know for certain. Some years later, after Mamie's husband and sons died and she moved here, she enlisted my help to find Charlese's son. He was born the year her family died. Keep in mind, this was before the internet made research easier."

He paused for another sip of water. "Eventually, our search led us to consider six boys born and adopted from Denton County during that year. Deeper investigation determined that, by that point, all were healthy, happy, eight-year-olds, loved by their adoptive families. Mamie longed to know if one of them was her sister's child, but refused to interrupt their lives by digging further. It was enough to know they were okay."

"Until one of them—me—came into foster care."

"Yes. Three years later. By then you were eleven, the same age her son, Brian Junior, was when he died. She was a spiritual woman and saw your matching ages as a sign. By then, she was heavily into the foster world with a house filled with teenagers. When she learned you were orphaned for the second time, she felt God leading her to bring you to Rosemary Ridge."

"She believed I was her nephew."

"She didn't know. We couldn't find out. The records were sealed. But Mamie *wanted* you to be, and she could not bear the thought of a little boy who could possibly be her nephew growing up alone."

"Why didn't she adopt me?"

"We discussed that extensively, and she was torn. If she had told you about her sister or if she'd adopted only you, what about the other boys in her care? Wouldn't leaving them out worsen their feelings of rejection? Those were Mamie's concerns."

"Why didn't she get a DNA test done on me?"

"She never said, but I strongly suspect she did not want a DNA test to disprove what she wanted to believe."

"That I was her biological kin."

Buckner tilted his head in agreement. "Now, you see why you're in the will."

Slowly, John-Parker nodded, his chest full of so much emotion he could hardly speak.

No matter how he'd hurt her, Mamie had loved him like the nephew she'd considered him to be.

It was enough to clog a man's throat.

He cleared it, aware that his insides trembled even as he outwardly maintained a businesslike calm.

"Why didn't you tell me any of these things before?"

"She asked me not to." Buckner held up a long-fingered hand. "Before you ask, I don't know why. People do strange things sometimes. Mamie had her ways and her reasons, most of which she took with her to the grave. As much as I respected and liked her, I did not always agree with her. As her lawyer, however, my duty was to comply with her wishes."

John-Parker understood. Mamie could be as stubborn as he was.

Was that a family trait?

"What happened to the sister, Charlese?" He couldn't bring himself to say "birth mother," since he might never know for certain.

Lonnie Buckner sighed. He lifted his fingertips from the desktop and dropped them again as if considering carefully before he spoke. "Charlese is another reason Mamie didn't tell you anything when you were a teenager. Charlese passed away shortly after giving birth."

So why wouldn't Mamie want to tell him? "What happened? Complications of having…a child?" He'd almost said, "Of having me."

"An overdose of sleeping pills."

Zoey gasped. "She took her own life?"

The shock jolted through John-Parker like electricity. He wanted to howl in protest. Elbows to knees, he bent forward to rub both hands over his face, fighting to regain his composure.

He felt Zoey's small hand against his back as she began to rub gentle, soothing circles. Comforting. Kind. She couldn't know how much he needed her touch. But, oh, how, he appreciated it. Appreciated her.

He'd wanted to know the truth, but hadn't expected any of this. The woman who might have been his birth mother had killed herself. Was it because of him?

*Lord, I know You're here. My heart hurts. Give me Your peace.*

He sat for long moments while the others remained quiet, as if respecting his need to gather his thoughts. All the while, Zoey rubbed between his shoulder blades. Sweet, loving woman.

After a few breaths and prayers, the shaking inside began to ease. He lifted his head from his hands and sat back.

Zoey took his hand and laced their fingers together. She seemed to intuitively realize how much he needed her right then.

The lawyer watched him with compassion. "I realize this much information is overwhelming, John-Parker. You'll need time to digest what you've learned."

"For certain." He huffed a mirthless laugh. "Thank you for being open and honest. You've answered a lot of questions that have bothered me."

"Some of those answers are quite painful, I'm sure."

"A man is always better for knowing the truth."

"That's the reason Mamie left this information with me. You're a man now. If you asked, she wanted you to hear the facts, or at least as many of them as we know."

Dazed, his brain whirling, John-Parker rose and shook hands with the attorney. "Thank you, sir."

Mr. Buckner handed over the adoption papers. John-Parker took them, aware they meant so much more to him than before. Unanswered questions remained, but his adoptive mother and dad had wanted him. Had loved him. Mamie had loved him, too—or who she'd thought he was—enough to search.

"Are you okay?"

Zoey walked out into the morning sun holding John-

Parker's hand, intuitively aware that he needed human comfort. He appeared as composed as always, but she knew he had to be rocked by the information.

She was flabbergasted herself. The woman she'd thought she'd known so well had carried a lot of secrets.

"As Buckner said, a lot to process."

"Do you want to talk about it? I'll understand if you don't, but I'm here if you do."

His fingers flexed against hers. He glanced down at her from his height advantage before drawing her close to his side. Touching. Side to side. Hand in hand. His long strides slowed to keep pace with the rhythmic flow of her long sundress. Like a couple strolling a small-town street together.

Rachel Colter, about to enter Stroud's Pharmacy with her two children, waved hello.

In tandem, Zoey and John-Parker returned the greeting. They'd done that a lot lately. Responding together as if their minds were in sync.

"I'm not sure what to say at this point," he admitted as Rachel disappeared inside the store and they continued to the end of the street. Still holding hands. Still close.

"Are you disappointed?" They stopped at the curb where the truck was parked.

John-Parker withdrew his key fob and clicked the locks. "I shouldn't be. I should be glad to know something."

He walked her to the passenger side and opened the door, took her elbow and helped her up. "Thanks for coming along today."

She reached for the seat belt, rolling her eyes in self-mockery. "Not that I was useful in any way."

"Oh, you were useful." He smiled, his stormy eyes a little sad, a lot stunned. She saw in them the swirl of unanswered questions that would probably never be resolved. "I felt you there, Zoey. I felt your support. So, thank you."

From her high position in the truck cab, they were almost

face to face. She touched his cheek. "I didn't want to be anywhere else, John-Parker."

She loved being needed. Especially by this strong, self-reliant man.

"Be careful." He quirked one corner of his mouth. "You're getting soft on me. Next thing you know, you'll be signing over your half of the inheritance."

The sadness still clung to his eyes, so that Zoey knew the joke was forced, a tease to break the serious mood.

If he needed to pretend all was well, she'd do that for him. "In your dreams, buddy boy."

Dreams. Oh, these unrelenting dreams. When had they become so convoluted?

She wanted to share in John-Parker's dreams, all of them, including the home to honor Aunt Mamie. She wanted to secure her children's futures. And hers. But how did she make things work in a way that pleased everyone?

He rounded the truck and climbed in.

Starting the engine, John-Parker braced both hands on the steering wheel, stared out the windshield and said, "Charlese committed suicide. That's the hardest part to take. If she was my mother…" He let the thought drift away on a river of sorrow. "The rest was good. Informative. Helpful."

So, he did want to talk. He couldn't forget any more than she could. "Heartbreaking. I'm so sorry."

Needing to touch him again, she put a hand on his forearm.

"I know." He glanced down at the place where they connected and then up at her, any effort to joke gone, his eyes stormy again. "If I'm her son, and the odds are pretty good that I am, something about me sent her over the edge. Was it having me in the first place? Or giving me away?"

"There are other reasons why a person feels hopeless, John-Parker. She could have suffered postpartum depression."

"I don't know much about that."

"I do. It is a serious condition that sometimes happens to

new mothers. It's more than being sad for a day. It's dark and horrible, and lingers on and on."

He cocked his head to one side. The engine idled but they remained in the parking space. "Speaking from experience?"

"If my doctor hadn't recognized the symptoms, I can't say what I would have done. It was a scary time. I didn't even want to hold or feed my baby." Remembering those awful days, she dropped her head and twisted her fingers together in her lap, ashamed and heartsick for the way she'd treated an innocent baby. "My poor, precious little son, was stuck with me for a mother and Vic for a dad."

"Hey. Look at me, Zoey." John-Parker's voice pulled her attention to his handsome face, his kind gaze. "You're a good mother."

"I try to be, but I still feel guilty for those early days of his life. I knew very little about caring for a baby. My husband seldom came home. When he did, he was angry at me for being depressed. The house wasn't clean enough. His laundry wasn't done. Why couldn't I stop that kid from crying? His attitude made me more depressed. I had nowhere else to turn, no family or job skills. Add in the hormones and a new baby, and I wanted to disappear. Or sleep forever."

"That's scary."

"When I look back on it now, I shiver to think what might have happened if my doctor hadn't stepped in."

"You think Charlese had this kind of depression?"

"It's a possibility, John-Parker, and just as my depression was not Owen's fault, her suicide was not her baby's fault. Whoever that baby was."

"Still, suicide is tough news to hear. But at least we know now why I was included in Mamie's will." He flashed her an ornery grin, obviously trying to lighten the heavy mood. "And you can stop picking on me about it."

"Ha, ha. I'll stop if you will." Except, lately, he no longer questioned her inclusion.

"Deal. Now, let's go buy stuff."

"What?"

"Retail therapy. Isn't that what you ladies call shopping to elevate your mood?"

She managed a snicker. "You hate shopping."

"Not with you." He put the truck in gear and drove them to a furniture store in Centerville, where they selected furniture and accessories for the apartment.

She did her best to make him laugh, intentionally choosing garish, ugly items for him to dismiss.

"But they're on sale," she'd say, a hand to one hip and a grin on her face.

"You, Zoey Alaina, are a cheapskate."

"Frugal," she'd say every time.

With a mock scowl, he'd move to the couch or chair or bedroom suit she'd already swooned over. "Do you love this?"

"I do, but—"

He'd hold up his index finger. "No buts. We'll take it."

That's the way the entire shopping expedition went. If she liked an item that fit the dimensions and color scheme, he bought it, arranged delivery, and then they moved on to the next thing needed for the apartment.

By afternoon's end, the list was complete. He treated her to lunch, fed her bites of his dessert—the most massive ice-cream-topped chocolate cake she'd ever seen—and they laughed until their sides hurt at every little thing.

Not one word of his grief or disappointment; he seemed determined to make her day away from the children and with him memorable.

Except for Mamie, John-Parker Wisdom was the bravest, strongest, person she knew.

If she hadn't been in love with him before, she was by the time he took her home.

# *Chapter Fifteen*

Over the next few weeks, progress on the house picked up speed. Zoey and the kids moved into the apartment. Workmen swarmed the main and upper floors. The asphalt for the basketball half-court arrived and, by nightfall, a single goal stood tall at one end. Today had been drying time, much to the aggravation of River and Charlie.

When they arrived after summer school tomorrow afternoon, they'd find a basketball on the court, ready to play. John-Parker couldn't wait to see their faces and hear their whoops.

Now, as he dressed and prepared for tonight's final town council meeting before his time ran out, he thought about the boys and how he'd grown attached to them.

He'd already told the social worker River and Charlie would be his first choices for the home. If it happened. Neither had anywhere else to go except to the shelter they lived in now. He didn't want to disappoint them about Mamie's house, so he'd said nothing about his request or the people he'd interviewed as potential house parents. He'd seen the hope in their wounded eyes, the longing to belong there, and it killed him to know he might have to disappoint them.

They knew the town council had rejected John-Parker's request. Twice. Tonight was his last opportunity to change their minds, his last shot at making his and the boys' dreams come true. The boys knew the house might go up for sale. Yet they hoped.

The responsibility weighed heavily on John-Parker's shoulders. He'd started something here in Rosemary Ridge that he was unprepared to finish.

He needed to be in Phoenix, not here. Brandt was better at

the business end of the company, but he expected John-Parker to carry his weight. The federal judge he'd accompanied on vacations in the past was asking for John-Parker again. She wanted no one else. He wasn't oblivious. He knew the judge liked him and had asked him to be her "bodyguard date" on a number of enjoyable occasions. He liked her, too.

But not the way he liked Zoey. He smiled to remember the fun he'd had following her around a mall while she'd pretended not to care about pretty things, opting for practical instead.

He wanted her to have pretty things.

He'd take a peanut butter sandwich with Zoey over a fancy restaurant with someone else any day.

He sighed, straightened his tie in the mirror and examined his suit and boots. He'd come to Rosemary Ridge to play the hero to Miss Mamie.

Would he leave a bigger failure than ever?

The hourglass was almost empty. With only a few weeks remaining to finish the work, John-Parker juggled a dozen different plates as fast as he could. The renovations. Shopping, selecting, and ordering odds and ends for the property. Supervising River and Charlie. The Bible study he'd begun for the boys and a couple of neighbor kids who'd wandered over.

Not that John-Parker was complaining about the visitors or the Bible study. Eternal things came first.

The boys grumbled when he'd first suggested the idea of actually studying the Bible, but ultimately they'd agreed. Probably for the snacks and the dollar he paid for each chapter of the Bible they read. Zoey had called him a manipulator, but she'd laughed when she'd said it. He'd offered her the same deal. To his surprised delight, she'd taken him up on it. He owed her seventeen bucks.

He stared at his reflection, saw the storm clouds in his eyes. After he left, who would teach the boys about Jesus and help them discover the good he saw in them?

Would Zoey find another man to make her laugh and to play trucks with Owen and Olivia?

Carrying his troubled thoughts out the door, he drove to city hall. As he parked in the adjacent lot, the importance of tonight's meeting pushed thoughts of Zoey and the kids into the background.

Straightening his tie for the dozenth time, he walked toward the meeting place, focused on what he'd say.

If the council didn't drop the nuisance ordinance tonight, he'd be forced to give up and agree to sell the property.

Zoey would be happy. He'd go home to Phoenix. And that would be the end.

Except, he didn't want it to be.

Since their star-gazing night, he and Zoey were different. They were agreeing more, arguing less about the house. Twice, he'd taken her out to dinner without the kids, thanks to Taffy as babysitter. It was almost as if they were a couple.

Except, they couldn't be. Not permanently.

He'd keep moving, the way he'd done all of his life.

He held the door for an elderly couple and then entered, fighting for his usual calm, collected demeanor. John-Parker might be anxious but no one except Jesus and him needed to know.

Hadn't he prayed for guidance until he'd run out of words? God was with him, and the rest was in His hands.

A handful of people nodded as John-Parker settled on the front row directly facing the council members. Earl Beck didn't look at him. No surprise. John-Parker had tried and failed to talk to the man in private and make amends. Beck would not budge. John-Parker hoped the other council members would.

Mayor Ben Jones, still in his red firefighter shirt, called the meeting to order. After the obligatory reports, he got right to the first point on the agenda—John-Parker's request for approval.

As expected, Beck offered his objections. John-Parker answered questions and repeated his reasons for wanting Mamie's House of Hope. He even read from a list of statistics about the number of teenage boys languishing in the system, the numbers who succeeded with guidance, and those who floundered when left to their own devices.

"Caring adult mentors and positive direction make all the difference in a young man's life," he said. "I speak from experience."

The rest of the board seemed more amenable this time. Two of them made eye contact and even smiled when he mentioned that a kid with a basketball court and a workshop in the backyard was less likely to get in trouble.

The property didn't have the workshop yet, but if the council would waive the nuisance rule, the plans were ready and contractors tentatively scheduled.

As he spoke with his heart in his throat and sincerity in his voice, he heard the door behind him open and the shuffle of people entering. Turning his head slightly, he saw several less-than-friendly faces. His stomach knotted.

"Is that all you have to say, Mr. Wisdom?" Mayor Jones asked.

John-Parker looked back toward the council. "Yes, sir. Thank you for your consideration."

"I got something to say, Mayor." This from one of the newcomers who'd marched closer to the front.

"All right, Brad, make it short."

"We're asking for trouble if you let him bring a bunch of hoodlums into our neighborhoods. Ask him about that River kid."

"The board is aware that a juvenile was arrested for vandalism. Were you in charge of him, Mr. Wisdom?"

John-Parker shifted on his boots. "No, sir, not yet, but I'd like to be. River lives in the boy's shelter in Centerville."

"What's he doing running the streets of Rosemary Ridge?"

"A social worker brings him to Miss Mamie's property. He works for me part-time and we hang out some, toss around a ball, jog the track. He's attending my Bible study group, too." He was careful not to mention the money he paid them. "River's a good kid, but he needs guidance."

"Reform school, I'm thinking," Beck grumbled.

"He's probably the one who stole the Jennings's Weed-wacker," Brad said. "Him and those other kids running the streets like gangbangers. Like you said, not a one of them from Rosemary Ridge. The county comes over here and dumps their trouble on us."

"The way they did for years." Beck jerked a thumb toward John-Parker. "He was one of them. Now, he's back, bringing trouble with him. *Again.* I vote no."

The mayor sighed. Members of the council who'd smiled at John-Parker a few minutes ago now stared down at the table.

The dream of continuing Mamie's legacy and of finding redemption seeped away in the murmur of agreeing voices around him.

He was losing. Again.

John-Parker dropped his head, waiting for the board to vote one final time. He'd probably never had a chance for approval but had been too hardheaded to stop trying.

"Mr. Mayor, could I say something please?"

John-Parker whipped his head around. Zoey?

She must have come in with the other objectors.

Any thread of hope he'd clung to snapped and disappeared.

Mayor Jones waved a weary hand in her direction. "Might as well, Zoey, everyone else has had their say. I hope."

"Thank you." With a nervous glance at John-Parker, she came toward the front table. "This is a letter, signed by most of the residents of Wildwood Lane, the neighborhood where Mr. Wisdom wants to turn Mamie Bezek's house into a home for boys. They want to have a say about the nuisance ordinance."

The mayor took the letter and gave it a quick perusal.

John-Parker's heart felt as if it would shatter.

Even though he knew Zoey had her own plans for the

house, he hadn't expected this kind of public betrayal. Not after the tender moments they'd shared.

Behind him, Wink Myrick put a hand on his shoulder. "Stay strong, son. God works in mysterious ways."

John-Parker knew that to be true. Even as his chest ached, he tried to refocus his thoughts on the Lord. Tried, but struggled to find the peaceful center he'd preached about to Zoey.

"I think the rest of you need to see this." The mayor passed the letter down the row of council members. One by one, as they finished reading, all but Beck looked at John-Parker.

"Did you have anything else to add before we vote, Zoey?"

"Yes, sir, I do. Thank you."

She cleared her throat. Her fingers worked the gathers of her blue-flowered skirt. "In recent months I've come to know John-Parker Wisdom. Even though we have different ideas about what should be done with Mamie Bezek's house, he is a good man. The ugly words that have been spoken by certain people in this town are lies. I've heard those rumors and then listened to some of you here tonight say awful things to him. Shame on you. Shame, shame for passing judgment on a man you haven't bothered to know. John-Parker has done nothing but good since he's been back in Rosemary Ridge, and this town is better for it. Those children and my children are better for knowing him. That's all I have to say. Shame on you all."

"Hear, hear," Frank called from his seat in the row behind John-Parker.

"Frank—" Ben aimed his gavel in a warning "—you're out of order."

"Said what I meant. I'm done now."

A collective chuckle moved through the room.

"All right then, let's get this over with. Do I hear a motion?"

"I move we waive the nuisance ordinance and approve Mr. Wisdom's request," one of the council members said.

"I second."

"All in favor, raise your right hand."

Every hand but Beck's lifted.

"Motion carries. Mr. Wisdom, thanks to Miss Chavez and this letter, you can do as you please with Miss Bezek's property. Congratulations."

John-Parker blinked. His mind whirled. *What? How?*

A few grumbles erupted from the back. He heard the words *street rats* but he was too stunned and elated to be bothered.

Zoey? Zoey had done this? For him?

Wink leaned close to his ear. "Told you."

He turned and shook hands with the brothers. "Thank you. I'm grateful."

"We might have done a little talking, but we take no credit, son." Frank hitched his chin toward the woman standing next to the mayor and looking more beautiful than ever.

When she saw him staring, her heart-shaped chin lifted in determination, soft eyes glassy, as if she might cry.

He didn't want her to cry.

What had she done? Oh, what had she done?

As if in a trance, John-Parker rose and went to her. It was all he could do not to yank her into an embrace in front of everyone. "Zoey. What just happened? I don't understand."

"Taffy told me about the terrible things that were said to you at the first meeting. Back then, I didn't know you. I didn't care. I hoped you'd give up and agree to sell the house."

Needing to touch her, John-Parker placed a hand on each of her upper arms. "And now?"

"How dare anyone in this town speak to you or about you in that manner."

She was so adamant, and adorable, he couldn't help smiling. Zoey in his corner felt really, really good. "What about the letter? How did you make that happen?"

"I asked Mr. Buckner about that idiotic ordinance. He said if the majority of Mamie's neighbors approved of the foster home, the council couldn't legally invoke the nuisance ordinance."

She'd talked to the lawyer? About him? About the home she didn't want him to open? Even knowing she could lose the house, she'd stood up for him and the foster home.

"You asked the neighbors to sign that letter, didn't you?"

She sniffed and lifted her chin higher, sassy-like. "Of course I did. What kind of friend would I be if I let a friend be treated so badly. You and the boys didn't deserve to be put in the same category as *hogs*." She made a growling sound. "That was plain mean. When I told the neighbors what happened, they agreed. Only Jane Renfroe shut the door in my face. Everyone else was nice."

"Why? Without that letter, you would have won. The decision to sell the house would be a done deal."

Her chin trembled. "I know."

She'd been on the cusp of having him and his big ideas out of the way and yet she'd rallied the neighbors on his behalf.

He didn't understand.

"Which means you and I are at odds again, fighting over the house. I don't want that anymore, Zoey. I want—" He stopped and rubbed a hand over his face. He'd almost made a dangerous declaration. He and Zoey lived in different states. He traveled too much. His occupation was hazardous.

Finally, he ended by saying, "I want you and those kids to be taken care of. I want you to be happy, too."

"And I want to make a difference in boys like River and Charlie. So I prayed." She gave his shoulder a little push. "Don't look so shocked. God and I are friends now, thanks to you and Mamie's Bible. Then I sought good counsel, like you said, and I believe you're right. Mamie's house should go on nurturing kids. Mamie would want that more than anything."

John-Parker's insides quivered. His mouth went dry. "You're giving up the house? Just like that? No more argument?"

"I'm trading my dream for yours."

John-Parker saw the moisture in Zoey's soft brown eyes, heard the passion in her voice, and knew how great a sacrifice she had made tonight. For him. And a group of boys she didn't know yet.

"I won't leave you with nothing," he said, vehement. "You have to know me better than that by now. Whatever funds we have left from the remodel are yours. Eventually, I'll buy out your half. Not all at once. I don't have that kind of money, but I'll make payments—"

She pressed three fingers against his mouth and hushed him. "We'll work things out, John-Parker. Isn't that what the Bible says? If we make the God choice, everything will work out for our good."

He saw the peace in her eyes and heard the determination in her voice. His soul soared at her restored faith in God. And in him.

*Thank You, Father. Thank You.*

Tonight she'd given him two gifts, and he was too grateful for words.

Not caring now who saw them, John-Parker drew her against his rampaging heart.

He didn't kiss her then, but he would. Oh, yes, he would.

She'd probably lost her mind in addition to the house and any hope for a secure future. Right now, though, the joy and relief on John-Parker's face kept Zoey from crumbling into panic mode.

She loved him. Love meant doing what was best for the other person even if it cost her something. Mamie's life had taught her that, and the Bible said the same thing.

If God wanted her to do this, He'd make a way for her and her children. Wouldn't He?

She was scared to trust, but the decision was made. Mamie's House of Hope would be a reality.

As she and John-Parker walked out into the dark parking lot together, hand in hand, he kept her close at his side. Zoey didn't resist, didn't want to. Even though his actions were gratitude and excitement over the house, she'd enjoy the moments while they lasted.

If she'd begun to wish they were a couple, she'd remind herself of his other life. He was a successful businessman who wanted to be anywhere but here. She was a college dropout with two kids, a failed marriage, and nothing to offer a wonderful man like John-Parker except her share in Mamie's house.

His lifestyle and hers did not mesh, no matter how much she loved him.

In a few weeks, he'd be gone. She tried not to think about that now.

John-Parker walked her to her car and opened the driver's door. When she started to climb in, he tugged her back into his arms.

Around them, car doors slammed, headlights flared, and the small crowd drove out of the lot, leaving them alone.

"At last." John-Parker bent his head to kiss her. Only this time, the kiss was deeper, sweeter, and lingered much longer than ever before.

Zoey let herself enjoy the kisses. He was grateful. That's all.

If tears welled in her eyes at the beauty of being held by John-Parker and in the knowledge of how much she'd miss him when he left, she didn't care.

At last, he eased away, as reluctant as she, but remained close enough to kiss again if the urge returned. Even if his kisses were gratitude, she needed them. They warmed a place in her heart that had slowly frozen during the years with Vic. She hadn't realized how cold she'd become on the inside until John-Parker had melted the iceberg inside. He'd taught her to trust again, to believe in God again.

She'd mourn when he left, but she would not regret their time together. She'd remember what it felt like to love and trust a man the way she loved and trusted John-Parker.

She and the children would be all right. For now, she had

the apartment and she'd remain until all the boys were placed and full-time house parents hired.

The leftover inheritance funds would hopefully be enough to tide her over for a while. She'd have time to find a better-paying job. Then she'd start all over again, taking nothing but good memories from this house.

"I have to go," she said at last. Taffy was at home with the little ones.

"I'll follow you."

Ever the protector. Except, he wouldn't be there much longer to protect any of them.

Shaking her head, she slid behind the wheel.

"No need. I'll see you tomorrow." She touched his freshly shaved face, longing for more than protection from her bodyguard. "Good night."

John-Parker leaned down to kiss her again, hovering just above her lips, his eyes studying hers. In the shadowy dashboard lights, she saw something in his expression that made her yearn. For the impossible.

He opened his mouth to say something but closed it again before finally saying, "Thank you."

Then he straightened, closed the door, and remained standing in the darkness as she pulled away and left her heart behind.

She let the tears she'd held back all evening slide down her cheeks.

Thanks was all she would ever get from her bodyguard.

# *Chapter Sixteen*

An elated John-Parker jogged to his truck and drove the few blocks to his rental. His plans for Mamie's legacy could finally fall into place. The house, the workshop, the remaining DCS paperwork. In a few weeks, he'd head back to Phoenix knowing he'd made a difference in the lives of boys like him.

Zoey and the kids would be okay. He'd return from time to time to see them and check in on the home.

They'd make phone calls, video chats. Stay in touch. Remain friends. Maybe she'd come to Phoenix and he'd show her the city and the beauty of the desert.

"Yeah." He rubbed a hand over his chest and realized he'd gone from thrilled to sad at the thought of leaving them behind.

He'd never felt that way about anyone. Never wanted to remain in one place before.

As he parked outside the B & B and started to get out, something stopped him. The uneasy feeling he got on assignment that warned him to be cautious.

Scanning the area, nothing seemed out of place. No one lurked about. The neighborhood was quiet.

Nonetheless, John-Parker retreated to the truck to watch and wait. When nothing moved, he texted Zoey to be sure she'd made it safely home. She didn't reply.

His body tensed.

He tapped the call icon. She didn't answer.

She was probably busy with the kids or in the shower.

He started the truck and headed for Mamie's house. Just in case.

Halfway there, his text went off.

One glance at the message and he shoved the accelerator to the floor.

* * *

The Rosemary Ridge emergency room was small but busy as John-Parker raced through the door and searched the waiting room chairs for a familiar face.

Taffy rose to meet him, a crying Olivia on one hip.

Owen slammed into his legs, lips quivering. "Mom got hurt."

John-Parker pressed the boy to him and spoke to Taffy over his bed-rumpled head. "What happened? Is Zoey all right? Where is she? I should have been with her."

Taffy put a hand on his arm to slow the spate of questions. "The doctor is treating her now. Her head was bleeding pretty badly—"

His anxiety skyrocketed. "Bleeding? What happened? A car wreck?"

Taffy bounced the still-wailing Olivia. "Someone was outside the house when she got home. When Zoey saw what they were doing and tried to stop them, they attacked her."

"Attacked?" John-Parker's voice rose. His fingers curled into fists. "Who? Did you see who did this?"

Taffy shook her head. "I heard her scream and by the time I got upstairs and out on the lawn, they were gone. You won't like what they did to the house."

"Forget the house," he growled. "Where's Zoey?"

"The nurse said to wait here."

"Too bad." Before she could stop him again, he charged through the closed double doors and into a long hall with rooms on each side.

"Can I help you?" A pink scrub-clad nurse, clipboard in hand, came around a desk.

"Where's Zoey Chavez?"

"Exam Room 2." She pointed. "You can wait outside the door, if you like."

No, he couldn't. He had to see her. Now!

John-Parker shoved open the heavy door to Exam Room 2. Blood didn't normally bother him. Hers did.

Zoey sat on the side of an exam table, with blood on her face, her hands and her pretty blue-flowered sundress.

A nurse stood at a sink running water into a plastic pan. She looked up. "Sir, we're almost finished. You can wait outside."

"No. I'm staying." John-Parker stalked to Zoey's side.

Her eyes and nose were red. She'd been crying. Scared. Bleeding.

"Who did this?" Somebody was going to pay.

Zoey lifted a bloody hand and touched his face. "You look so fierce. I'm okay."

"You're bloody. That's not okay."

"Sir," the nurse said, "if you'll wait outside, we'll get her cleaned up. The doctor has already stitched her wounds."

"Wounds? More than one? Where? Where are you hurt? I should have followed you home."

"A couple of small cuts, John-Parker. Nothing serious. I fell into that stack of leftover sheet metal."

His blood, hot a moment ago, ran ice-cold. "You didn't fall. Someone pushed you."

"Yes." Tears welled in her eyes. She was going to cry again and he was going to have to hurt someone. Bad. "They sprayed red graffiti on our beautiful new paint job. I tried to stop them and they pushed me."

The nurse approached with a rolling metal tray and the pan of water. "Sir."

Zoey looked at the nurse. "He can stay. Please. I need him."

That was all John-Parker had to hear. He wouldn't leave this ER without Zoey for a billion dollars. Or if his life depended on it.

Zoey was hurt and she needed him.

*Lord, I need her, too.*

*And you love her.*

Yes. Yes!

"Can I touch you? Will I hurt you if I hold you? I need to hold you."

“Sir, I need to clean her up so she can be discharged.”

“Get the paperwork ready.” He reached to take the pan. “I’ll do this.”

“No—” The nurse started to protest but Zoey interrupted.

“Do as he asks. I refuse any further hospital treatment. I want to go home. With him.”

With a disapproving set to her mouth, the nurse left the room.

As soon as the door closed, Zoey’s quavering voice whispered, “Hold me. Please hold me.”

As gingerly as if she were broken everywhere, John-Parker slid onto the exam table with her and pulled her against his heart. For the rest of his life, he’d remember the hospital and blood smell and the terrible realization that he could have lost her forever.

Life held no promises of tomorrow. If he left Rosemary Ridge for good, Zoey might not be there when he returned. Like Mamie.

And if something bad happened, as it had with Mamie, Zoey would never know how much he loved her.

Zoey listened to the rapid thud of John-Parker’s heart until her own wild pulse calmed enough to pull away.

“Thank you.” She licked dry lips and stared down at her bloody hands. “I should wash these.”

“Let me.” Before she could offer what would be a weak protest at best, he’d squeezed out the washcloth and began to wipe her face.

When he rinsed the cloth and bloodied the water, she shuddered. “I ruined your nice shirt and tie.”

He glanced down and shrugged, and then went back to washing her right arm and hand, as she would Olivia’s. Gently. Thoroughly.

“I don’t care about the shirt, Zoey. I care about you.”

He cared, but he was leaving her. Like everyone else.

“Don’t worry about the rest of the blood. I’ll shower when I get home. The house looks worse than I do.”

"No jokes." He gave her a fierce glare. "Did you see who did this?"

"One of them, for sure."

His jaw clenched. "Tell me."

At that moment, the nurse reentered the exam room with the discharge papers and a wheelchair. Zoey managed to sign the papers.

John-Parker grumbled when her fingers shook

"I'd push you out," the nurse said, "but I doubt this guard dog of yours will let me."

"I've got her. Thanks." As if she'd had major brain surgery or worse, John-Parker carefully helped Zoey off the table into the wheelchair. She'd remember this kindness, and the way she'd felt when he'd barreled into the room in full security-guard mode.

With the nurse walking alongside, he rolled her out into the waiting room.

She was instantly rushed by a toddler and her best friend.

"Mom, you got hurt." Owen's eyes were red from crying. She thought Taffy's were, too.

When she reached for her son, John-Parker stopped her with a hand to her shoulder and then lifted Owen onto her lap.

"I'm okay, baby. Just a scratch where I fell down." She glared a warning at John-Parker not to mention exactly how she'd fallen. "I got a Band-Aid. A big one!"

Owen's worried eyes brightened. "A Snoopy one?"

"Only big boys like you get Snoopy ones. Mine is plain old white. But, you know what? You've been so brave out here, I think we should stop for ice cream. What do you say?"

"Yes!" Owen threw his arms around her neck. She winced but snuggled him close.

John-Parker's sharp-eyed gaze saw the flinch of pain and said to Taffy, "Will you take the kids for ice cream while I take Zoey home and get her settled?"

Taffy stiffened. "Only if she says so."

Still shaky and with too much dried blood on her clothes

and in her hair to be seen anywhere, Zoey said, "I'd be grateful. John-Parker will take care of me." She said this with conviction. As long as he was here, her bodyguard would be on duty. Just like he would for anyone else.

Even if she was a silly woman with fantasies of love, tonight, she wanted to revel in his protective consideration.

Taffy looked her over and then looked to John-Parker. "I'm trusting you with her."

"I won't let you—or her—down." He lifted Owen from her lap, kissed him on the forehead, handed him two twenty-dollar bills, and told him to pay for the ice cream and to bring his mom a cup of Rocky Road.

Zoey's shaky insides smiled. He'd remembered her favorite.

With Owen encouraged and on a mission for his mom, Taffy took the two little ones and left.

John-Patrick rolled her wheelchair to his truck. Before she could even try to stand on weak wobbly legs, he swooped her into his powerful arms and slid her onto the passenger seat.

Leaning in, he kissed her and then, with all the seriousness of his occupation, whispered, "We have to talk."

"Okay."

But all the way home, he remained silent, pensive, his jaw tense, his eyes glued to the road ahead.

She was glad for the silence. Her thoughts were still a jumble. All she really wanted was a shower and more time with him. Then everything would be all right.

Except, it wouldn't be.

When the headlights swept across the front of the house, John-Parker growled, his hands tightening on the steering wheel.

"Who did this?"

"There were two of them, but I only saw one."

"Let me guess. Earl Beck."

She swallowed, the anxiety of that awful moment when

he'd shoved her rising again. "Yes. Now, we'll have to spend more money to repaint."

"I'll take care of this. You take care of you." He parked and came around the truck to help her out. Once more, he carried her.

She'd have protested except for the dizziness that had yet to subside. A minor concussion, the doctor had said. She wasn't sure she wanted to tell John-Parker. He looked dangerous enough from seeing the cuts.

When they got to the basement stairs, she said, "I can take it from here. Put me down."

He ignored the comment and didn't release her until they reached the apartment and her bedroom.

"Is there anything you need? Anything else I can do?"

"Wait for me in the living room?" She hoped he wouldn't leave yet.

"You got it. If you need anything, just holler."

He closed the door behind him, leaving her to shower in the en suite and change into clean clothes while he headed into the living room to protect her privacy. She loved how respectful he was.

She also loved his protectiveness, but she hoped he didn't go after Earl Beck tonight. He was too angry.

When she finished and made her way, slowly, from the back of the apartment to the living room, John-Parker stood at the island, two cups in hand.

"You had chamomile tea in the cabinet. I thought it might help."

She smiled and settled on the couch with a sigh. "It's perfect."

He handed her the warm cup.

"Thank you for this. And for rushing to my rescue." Her whole body hurt, but the headache was the worst.

His face clouded. "I should have followed you home."

"I wouldn't let you, remember?"

"Yeah. I didn't listen to my gut and you got hurt. I don't

like that." He sat down beside her and turned to watch, as if he feared she'd pass out any moment.

She was made of stronger stuff than that, although she'd admit tonight had been scary and when her head had slammed into the side of the house, she'd seen stars and black spots.

Sipping the hot tea, Zoey reminded herself to relax. The traumatic experience was over. She was okay now that her favorite bodyguard was hovering like a helicopter full of marines.

Setting the tea on the side table, she touched his tight jaw. "You look dangerous."

Fire shot from his eyes, lightning in the stormy gray. "I am dangerous, especially when it comes to you."

"That's nice to hear but—"

It was his turn to touch her. Fingertips against her lips, followed by a soft kiss, effectively silenced her.

"I have something important to say, Zoey. Something I realized tonight when I heard you were hurt."

"Okay." She shifted her sore body toward him, loving his ferocity for her and her children. Did he look this way for his clients?

He took a swig from his cup, set it aside, squeezed his top lip and stared at her bandaged head and arm for long, troubled moments.

Finally, when the tea had started to relax her tense muscles, he spoke.

"If anything happened to you, I'd be destroyed. I can't lose you."

Her muscles tensed up all over again. He couldn't mean that the way it sounded.

"You're a good man."

"I'm a desperate man who doesn't know how all this can work out, but I love you, Zoey. I can't leave Rosemary Ridge without you knowing."

So, he loved her, but he'd still leave her?

Wasn't that a kick in the teeth?

Head throbbing harder, she fought the urge to spill her

feelings all over him. Love, she'd learned, was never enough for anyone to stay.

"I understand. We can never work out." She sounded as cold as she felt.

He took her hands and stared into her face. "Why not?"

"We're a summer romance, a fling. I get it."

His forehead furrowed into a scowl. "What are you talking about?"

"Us. You and me. You say you love me. And I love you, but in less than a month, you'll leave Rosemary Ridge and I'll be forgotten. You'll be in Arizona or somewhere trying to get yourself killed. We'll never work."

He fell back against the couch cushions. "It's my job, isn't it? You're afraid of my job."

"I'm afraid of losing you. One way or the other..."

"And I'm afraid of losing you." He tugged her back so that their faces were inches apart. "Let's not do that."

His look was tender, melting.

"Can we?" Her voice quivered and tears threatened. She desperately wanted to believe they could work things out.

"With God's help, we'll find a way." He cupped her cheek. "I love you, Zoey. I've never said that to any woman. So, if you love me, don't be afraid. We have something special. Let's keep it going. Forever. You, me, the kids. Maybe more kids, if you want them, too."

Her pulse ratcheted up, hopeful, but afraid to believe. "Is this a proposal?"

"Yes, ma'am." His thumb rode the soft skin beneath her chin, tantalizing, tender. "Should I get on one knee? Or wait for a better time and place? Whatever you want."

"This is the place and now is the time. I love you, John-Parker Wisdom, and I accept. No need to kneel. Just seal it with a kiss. Make me believe this is real."

His mouth curved. And he did exactly that.

# *Epilogue*

On a cool November day with fiery autumn leaves still clinging to the maples, John-Parker Wisdom greeted visitors to the official dedication of Mamie's House of Hope. Dignitaries from the city and state admired the spaces that would soon be home to six teenage boys, including River and Charlie. Today, the well-groomed boys wore shiny new boots he'd bought for them. Even River looked happy as he showed visitors around the property with proud stories of the work he and Charlie had done themselves. They were especially excited to show off the workshop and greenhouse where they'd learn building and mechanic skills and how to grow their own food.

"Sweat equity is good for the soul." Zoey stood next to him, even prouder than the boys. "You've done well, Mr. Wisdom."

"You, too. Now, if I can get you married by Christmas and get moved out of that rental, *all* my dreams will be fulfilled."

"You're still sure about living here? Confident you can run your business from Rosemary Ridge?"

They'd had this conversation before. She knew his decision, but seemed to need reassurance that he wouldn't bolt. Time, he prayed, would heal her fear of abandonment. Her love had healed so much in him that he hadn't realized still hurt.

"As long as you don't mind a trip to Arizona now and then, Brandt agrees we can make this work. We *will* make it work, Zoey. You and me. I can't do life without you."

The worry in her eyes disappeared. Since the night of her injury and his awakening to love, their devotion and trust had grown. He'd brought Earl Beck and his vandalizing son to justice, and the judge had ordered restitution, requiring them to repaint the house. Someday, John-Parker hoped to win the man over. Someday.

He paused to greet a newcomer and thank him for a generous donation. The house swarmed with bigwigs and ordinary folks who cared about kids. Senators, celebrities, clients, Wink and Frank, the Colters, Doc Howell, neighbors and acquaintances came to admire, affirm and donate. Clare and Taffy weren't the only media people on hand.

They'd filed for a 501c charity exemption with the IRS and were soliciting donations from every wealthy client who'd ever used his security services. Between the state and federal funds, grants and donations, the house would prosper. So would he and Zoey and the boys they raised together in this house.

Even his rapper client, Mo Rich, had shocked him with a generous donation and a note stating he wished someone had done this for him when he was running the streets.

"You never know what's deep inside people," Zoey had said. "Everyone's redeemable."

This from the woman who'd doubted.

When she turned back from speaking with a neighbor, smile warm, John-Parker bent to kiss her, quick and light. He couldn't get enough of her. God had given him this generous, caring woman and John-Parker was still amazed at his capacity for love. Love for her, for Owen and Olivia, for the teenage boys. Sometimes emotions threatened to leak out of his eyes. He was that fulfilled.

Mamie would be pleased. And he could rest in knowing he'd done all he could to redeem himself.

The only thing missing on this perfect day was for Brandt to attend. He'd been invited but had declined, sending a donation instead. John-Parker understood his aversion, but he'd wanted his approval. In person. Something he wouldn't get.

"Keep the faith," Zoey whispered as she held his suit-clad arm.

"He won't change his mind. This town hurt him too deeply."

"You, too, but you're here and planning to stay." She lifted her beautifully interesting face to him. "Have I told you in the last five minutes how much I love you and I can't wait for Christmas to get here so I can be your wife?"

"We don't have to wait."

Her mouth curved. "But I want a Christmas wedding. You, me, the kids, and Jesus, starting our lives together under the mistletoe and tinsel."

Smile as tender as his mushy insides, he gazed down at her lips. "Wishing for that mistletoe right now."

But if she wanted a Christmas wedding, she'd have one with all the trimmings.

"You'll be the best Christmas present I've ever gotten." She tiptoed up to kiss his cheek. "But I have an early one for you."

"No gifts needed. I already have everything. You, the kids, Mamie's house, a great job."

Holding his hand and smiling, she rotated him toward the entrance to Mamie's House of Hope. "Merry early Christmas, my love. He promised me."

Joy, already overflowing, rocketed through John-Parker. For there, standing in the doorway, looking lost and nervous, was his best friend, his brother, his business partner.

Brandt James had faced his dread and come to Rosemary Ridge.

For him.

John-Parker looked at his future bride, awareness seeping in. "You did this?"

"I helped a little, but he's here for you, John-Parker. The same as all these other people who love and admire you."

Holding tight to Zoey's hand, heart soaring, John-Parker went to greet the one man he'd never expected to step foot into this dream of his.

And now his dream and Zoey's was truly complete.

* * * * *

Dear Reader,

In our family, foster and adoption are big deals. By most recent count, we have eight adopted children in our immediate family, six of those from foster care. So, it was only fitting at some point that I write about adults who grew up in foster care without ever having a permanent family to call their own.

*Redeeming the Past* is the first book in the new *House of Hope* series about three former foster brothers who return to Rosemary Ridge, Oklahoma, to lay their pasts to rest. (And of course, to meet their one true love along the way!)

If you've read my book, *A Mommy for Easter,* you've already met some of the citizens of Rosemary Ridge. I hope you enjoy visiting them again. In *Redeeming the Past*, you'll meet new characters, too, including now successful security specialist, John-Parker Wisdom and widowed Zoey Chavez and her two small children. Sparks will fly, opinions will conflict, but God has a plan to set both these lonely hearts into a loving family.

I love hearing from readers. Feel free to contact me at Linda@lindagoodnight.com where you can also subscribe to my occasional newsletter.

Happy Reading!
*Linda Goodnight*